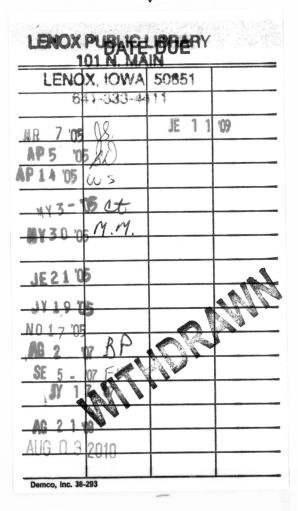

INADMISSIBLE: LOVE

INADMISSIBLE: LOVE

•

Donna Wright

AVALON BOOKS
NEW YORK

PRINTED IN THE UNITED STATES OF AMERICA
ON ACID-FREE PAPER
BY HADDON CRAFTSMEN, BLOOMSBURG,
PENNSYLVANIA

For Lynn and Ben,
who often wonder if I'm ever coming out of the
office.

Acknowledgments

So many people helped make this book possible, I'm afraid I'll miss someone. Jesus Christ, Who died that I may live. My mom who would have been so proud were she still with us. My dad who has made plans on what to do with the money. Mary, Doyle, Tim, Sandy, and Ashley. I love you all. The Smoky Mountain Romance Writers, especially the "old guard" who all started out together and keeps plugging on. Leanne, Katie, Teresa, DML, Kerri (will you please quit saying "Told you so?") and all the others whom I love. Thank you for sharing in my joy. To those published authors who have shown me such kindnesses, including Brenda Mott, Karen Hawkins, Cheryl Wolverton, Debra Dixon and Sherilyn Kenyon. To the "Faithful Five," for believing in me, I still have the pen. Beverly, and "the other Donna," who keep me grounded and remind me writing isn't the whole world. Cornerstone Church for their love and support. Crystal, who makes all the accomplishments real with three words, "You go, girl!" And, my sometimes writing-partner, Sharon Griffith, without whose "tweaking" this book would not have been possible.

Chapter One

Her pager picked the wrong moment to sound—the loud sharp noise filled the small room. Now, a dilemma presented itself to Danni Price. She checked the display on the pager, saw her office number and spoke to the young man before her, "I'll take a scoop of French Vanilla and one of Chocolate Fudge."

As she accepted the cup, she took her phone from her purse and dialed her office. "Yeah, Bonnie, what's up?"

"Your mother called and wanted to know where you are."

"I'm on my way to the auction right

now. If she calls again, tell her I'm not going to stand her up. I'll be there." Danni slammed the phone shut and rolled her eyes.

She could understand her mother's paranoia as she walked down the street. Danni's sister had already invented a reason not to be a part of the literacy auction.

Danni, however, had more guts. She'd promised her mother she'd do it, so she would.

She dreaded it. Every Flag Day the Literacy Foundation would ask people to supply goods and services for auction. But, like every thing else in life, there was that infamous catch.

The Ramsey Restaurant donated dinner as "bait." Danni held the advertisement during the auction and would eat with whomever held the highest bid.

Last year, she'd bid on a guy who publicized for a motorcycle shop. A nice ride, even if the guy wasn't her type.

Since this year she'd again gotten suckered into all the hoopla, she enlisted the aid of her closest colleague at the firm. Hugh Cramer and she put together a little over five hundred dollars. With those funds he would buy the restaurant certificate and her company for the evening. In the past few years, the Literacy Foundation's auctions seldom sold anything for more money.

She smiled and entered the main branch of the Fort White Public Library. After Hugh outbid all comers, she'd be able to address all the work that awaited her in her briefcase. The benefits would be for the Literacy Foundation. She could please her mother, Hugh would get a great dinner, and she'd get home before nine.

No plan could be more perfect.

Her mother brought her out of her reverie. "Danielle Price, I told you to wear that summer dress I bought for your birthday."

"I'm a working girl, Mother, this business suit is my work clothes." She almost wished she'd listened to her mother. With so many people gathered, the room was warm.

Claudette Price gave Danni a look that brought back childhood memories. Fortunately, the adult Danni didn't face cleaning the utility room as punishment. "I want you to bring a high price tonight," her mother continued.

"You told me they weren't bidding on

me. It's the foundation that's important, remember? And, thanks again, Mom for volunteering me for this."

"I potty-trained you, Danielle. You owe me." Claudette pulled on the hem of Danni's jacket, straightening her clothes as one would a child. As a teacher, her mother always worked with the literacy project. In fact, Danni couldn't remember a time when she'd not been a part of it.

"Sold to the highest bidder!" Judge Thomas Cole's voice sounded throughout the large main area of the building. Tall and thin with graying hair, Judge Cole had not resided over Danni's cases to this point. The respect his reputation commanded still made her uneasy, like meeting a third grade teacher for the first time.

Tugged along by her mother, Danni soon found herself next in line. She could feel her blood pressure rising, her face getting hot. Impelled by her mother's nudge, Danni mounted the steps to the makeshift stage, and came to a stop next to the Judge.

She found it impossible not to return his disarming smile. "Miss Price is an attorney with Smelcer and Greene, who just won a very big case." Since that litigation had been against the Judge's son-in-law, Danni cringed as he spoke. "Second, The Ramsey Restaurant donated two steak dinners. Now, between this beautiful woman with her big brown eyes and hair like black silk and a mouthwatering steak, we should see some high figures for the foundation. What say you, my friends, what's the first bid?"

She relaxed as Hugh called out, "I'll give one hundred dollars."

Silence followed Hugh's bid. No other bids for a long moment. Good, not only would she get out of this, she'd get out of it cheap.

The Judge picked up his gavel to call an end to the bidding.

A voice sounded from the back of the area. "Two hundred dollars."

Danni strained to see who'd made the bid. She could discern a movement as a tall man started his trek toward the front.

Hugh didn't hesitate. "Three hundred dollars." She found him among the audience and smiled.

The stranger made his way toward the stage, stopped short of climbing the stairs and took an empty seat in the front row.

She regarded him with curiosity as his

mouth quirked with amusement. He was thin but muscular; blue eyes met hers from beneath dark lashes and his jet-black hair was cut short as the style of most businessmen.

His deep voice reverberated through the room as it rolled over her in waves. "I'll give five hundred dollars." A hush fell over the room. The bids were usually placed in fifty-dollar and one hundred-dollar increments. She glanced at the Judge, who didn't seem to care that this man, even with his good looks, just broke one of the unspoken rules.

This could be bad.

Danni looked for Hugh. He sat at his table counting the money. She worried when even change piled around the bills he handled. This could get worse before it got better.

The Judge's voice rang out, "We have five hundred!"

"Five-fifty!" Hugh had enough, thank God.

"Six hundred dollars." The man stood and strolled to a case of books, lazing against it, blue eyes full of humor and a cocky grin she wanted to smack off his face.

The Judge made the call, eyeing Hugh. "We have six hundred, want to go for seven?"

Hugh's gaze turned to Danni who nodded. She would have to pawn the dog, but she wasn't going out with this guy.

Hugh rang out, "Seven hundred."

Excitement rose throughout the crowd. The higher the bid, the more money the foundation received.

The warmth in Danni's face grew to a red-hot blaze.

The stranger began to look more familiar as he tilted his head to one side, as if deciding if she were worth the price he would have to pay.

The Judge called, "Seven hundred, want to go for eight, Mike?"

Mike? Something clicked in her mind. *Oh, no.* That's why she knew his face. This little bidding war must be intended to embarrass her in front of the audience, who happened to be the local bar association. She'd practiced law for only a year, and Mike's father, a seasoned veteran, lost a big case to her last week. She'd seen him several times in the courtroom and in the

Sommers' office for meetings. Why hadn't she recognized him before now?

Mike's words brought her to the painful moment. "Eight hundred."

Danni signaled Hugh, again. *I'll have to sell the car.* "Okay, nine hundred!" Hugh shouted to the Judge.

"One thousand!" This was the highest bid of the evening. The crowd applauded as Danni squirmed with embarrassment.

For a third time, Danni signaled Hugh, this time, not caring if someone noticed her nod. What loan company would give her a second mortgage on the house?

"Eleven hundred!" Hugh yelled. *Why couldn't he have just bid one thousand fifty?*

Michael straightened from his place against the books. With narrowed eyes, he considered his opponent. "Mr. Cramer, let's just get this over with, shall we? Fifteen hundred!"

The room let out a collective gasp, and then applauded Michael. Danni knew she couldn't top that bid.

Picking up the gavel, the Judge called out the final bid, "Fifteen hundred going once!"

Danni quelled an urge to throw up.

"Going twice!"

Michael Sommers, however, looked pleased with himself.

"Gone! To my grandson, Michael Sommers."

Though the gavel hit the lectern to indicate the end of the bidding war, Danni stood for a moment to gather her wits and put down the sign she'd been holding as the advertisement for The Ramsey.

As her date went to pay his fee, Hugh approached and took her hand as she descended the three steps that led from the temporary stage erected for the function.

"Sorry, Danni."

"Think." She urged him, repressing panic. "I'm not going out with this guy. Do you know his reputation? He's always looking for a new woman to conquer."

"Danni, you have no choice. He just paid fifteen hundred dollars for the pleasure of your company."

Since Danni had been the last participant auctioned, the attendees milled around. Some paid for their services while others straightened hair or lipstick or helped with the cleanup.

Danni wanted to stomp her feet, but knew making a scene was out of the question. Instead, she glared at Hugh. "Let me make myself clear. The devil will be wearing bunny slippers when I go out with the likes of Michael Sommers."

Hugh looked past Danni and extended his hand. "Mike, good to see you."

Danni whirled around to see Michael standing behind her. She was sure he'd heard what she said.

Michael exchanged pleasantries with Hugh, then asked Danni, "Do we need to stop by the shoe store before leaving for the restaurant?"

"Um. No. Actually, I have some briefs in the car and I'll need to get them to look over while we eat."

"I don't think so. You see, I paid for this date, and you're going to talk to me."

She managed a response through stiff lips. "Okay. What about this? I pay you five hundred down, right now. And, a hundred dollars a month until the date is paid for."

Her reply must have amused him. "How about *this?* We leave now and when we get to the restaurant, we talk and act like we know each other?"

"We both know why you did this. Your firm is angry because I won the case last week."

His patronizing tone angered her more. "Actually, I participate every year in the literacy auction. It may shock you to know my actions don't revolve around you. Now, if we need to go buy bunny slippers, fine, but otherwise, my car is out front." He turned to Hugh. "Good to see you."

With a sheepish grin for Danni, Hugh left them alone.

Michael Sommers drove Danni to The Ramsey on the other side of Fort White. The drive took about twenty minutes and for the life of her Danni couldn't think of a word to say to him.

He apparently tried to put her at ease with light conversation and Danni answered any questions with one-word answers.

Before they got out of the car, however, Michael turned to her. "I don't know what you know, or I guess I should say, what you think you know, but I really would like for us to have a nice time tonight."

Danni's temper flared. "Then you should have let me buy the date, go home, and look over my work. I'm not interested in you, Michael."

"You know, Danielle, we could be friends. I'm not asking you to marry me, just to get along for the next couple of hours."

Danni thought about it. "For literacy. For the next two hours, we're friends."

Chapter Two

When the steaks arrived, Danni checked her watch. She knew she would be competing with him in future cases and couldn't think of what to say that would give him an indication of what to expect from her.

No problem. She'd keep him talking. This kind of man always liked to hear his own voice.

"So," Michael handed the waiter his menu after ordering a steak, "Did you grow up in Fort White?"

The waiter also took her menu. "The Norwood area. In fact, I own the house where my mom grew up. I inherited it from my grandmother. I bought my brother and sister's share, actually." *This is so nerve-racking. He's the enemy and I have to stay on guard every minute.* "I assume since the firm was established before either of us were born that you also grew up here."

"Out West, before it grew into the strip mall paradise it is today."

She nodded, not really knowing if she should answer him or just sip her water. She chose the latter.

After a long look around the restaurant her eyes settled on him. *This would be the type of place a man like Michael Sommers would take a real date.* The tables had nice linen cloths and napkins, and was lit by candlelight. There weren't so many of them that she felt like she should answer the people at the next table when a question was asked. All in all, she liked The Ramsey.

Now, Michael Sommers was another matter, altogether.

Up close and with his jacket off due to the warm summer evening, she could tell more about him. He didn't look so much like an attorney without the coat. She admitted his blue eyes always gleamed like he had a secret. His jet-black hair was about the color of hers.

Danni broke the uncomfortable silence. "I know this may sound like a pick-up line, but do you come here often?"

He put his water glass down after a long drink. "Yeah, I do. It's one of my favorites. Their steaks can't be beat and shrimp night makes my mouth water just to think about it."

"I like shrimp. Broiled, though, or in a cocktail, I don't like the breaded kind."

"I'll keep that in mind." He arched a brow. Danni found it made him even more handsome. "Tell me, Danni, how do you like practicing law?"

She picked up her napkin and laid it in her lap. "It's different."

He followed suit. "In what way?"

The waiter brought their drinks, both colas.

After he left the table, Danni answered Michael. "I wanted to save the world, but right now I get mostly divorces and bankruptcies. It's all just a matter of paperwork."

"That's the way most of us start out. It'll get more interesting as you go."

"I hope that's true, especially after winning the case last week—" she stopped short, helpless to halt her discomfort. "That was not meant as a slam."

He waved his hand in a gesture of dismissal. "None taken. You won a big case and it *will* impact your career."

"Maybe we shouldn't talk about cases, anyway, since we aren't working together." What cologne did he wear? It weaved its way around her.

"No, we're not. But, I just got word that you're taking Sallie Fairmont as a client."

Their salads arrived at the table, along with bread and other condiments. The waiter withdrew as quietly as he came.

Danni stared at him. "How do you know that?"

His smile, though devastatingly white against his tanned skin, left her ill at ease. "Because Fairmont Farms has been with our firm for years and Joe called me today to tell me you're the other lawyer involved."

Danni thought a long moment; maybe this was Mr. Tall, Dark, and Handsome's way of getting into her head on the Fairmont case. "Tell me what you plan to do with it."

He looked at her, blue eyes dancing. "Let's just say I have a few tricks up my sleeve that will leave you breathless." *That* she could believe. As a matter of fact, just looking at him was leaving her a bit breathless even now.

She continued as if unaffected by his cologne, his eyes, and the longing that he should at least hold her hand. "I don't think you can do much to me on a divorce case. My concern is for my client's well being, and the care of her child. Show me the money, we'll look at any offers."

"Big Joe says he wants that little boy. What're the odds?"

A little off kilter just because she wasn't accustomed to such a dynamic date, Danni hesitated, "Well, let me see . . ."

She couldn't stop staring at him. His compelling blue eyes captivated her, even as his firm mouth curled as if always on the edge of laughter.

Pulling her out of her examination, Michael asked, "Are we back to bunny slippers?"

She had to laugh, though it was more

nervous than sarcastic. "I'm afraid so." She went into business mode. "And, Michael, be honest, you know the Judge will give us custody. I'll let you approach us with support and visitation."

"That's not going to happen, counselor."

"Regardless of the money Big Joe may have, he's not getting this kid. A child this age should be with his mother."

"If his mother isn't fit—" Michael quit talking, and muttered something under his breath.

Like lightning, realization coursed through her. She leaned forward on the table to give her words emphasis. "You're going to try prove my client unfit? Sallie Fairmont? Come on, Michael."

For just an instant, something lit his eyes that looked like confusion. "Are you familiar with Mrs. Fairmont?"

She shrugged to hide her insecurity. "Other than the fact she's my client, no."

"I didn't think you two ran in the same circles. Just can't see you hanging out at Temptation Alley." He named one of the seediest bars in town.

"Sallie Fairmont? You can't be talking

about elegant, always manicured, Sallie Fairmont?"

Michael nodded and took a bite of a tomato.

"The same lady who asked me not to choose a restaurant that served wine when we met to discuss this case? You must be mistaken."

"I'll bet you custody of Little Joey."

She smirked so he wouldn't see her lack of confidence. "You think you can prove my client unfit, and get custody of the minor child for Mr. Fairmont?"

Michael leaned back from the table. "In a word, yes."

She raised her glass in a toast to their challenge. "You're on, Mr. Sommers, I'll see you on the courthouse steps."

Michael raised his glass in acquiescence, but didn't drink when Danni did. For just a moment he girded himself with resolve. "Danni?"

She stopped and looked at him. *God, he liked the way her hair shimmered.* "Yes?"

He paused, finding the right words. "We're attorneys. When I'm in that courtroom, you're just another lawyer. One with beautiful brown eyes, but just another lawyer all the same."

"I'll remember that when I'm winning cases against you in the future, Mr. Sommers."

Her smile touched him in a way he'd never thought a woman could. Until that moment, all women had been the same to Michael. He sipped his soft drink as the waiter brought the main course.

The rest of their time together, Michael tried to find fault with his date. The longer he spent with her, however, the more intrigued he became. *This will wear off by tomorrow.* He repeated the words to himself like a chant.

His cell phone rang. He smiled at her in apology and took the call. "Hello?"

His secretary answered him. "Mike, I'm sorry to bother you, but I have a problem."

He tried to sound nonchalant. "Oh? What's that?"

"Your court date on the Griffith accident has been moved to tomorrow. Are you ready for that, or do we need to go back to the office?" He could hear Karen's baby cooing in the background.

"No. We're ready on that."

"Are you with someone?"

"Yes."

"Okay, well I'll get that in the morning, sorry to have bothered you."

"No problem." He shut the phone and picked up his fork.

Danni smirked. "You can't even eat a meal without a call, can you Michael?"

"Get used to it. The price of a successful career."

"Or a full little black book?" She took a bite of her potato.

"No, Danni. Just my secretary." He took the woman to dinner, and she thought she had the right to question him about his relationships? He thought not. "What do *you* care?"

"That's the best part. I don't." A faint glint of humor lit her dark eyes. "I have to admit, the food is wonderful here."

The subject was dropped, but guilt plagued Mike. For the life of him, he didn't know why.

By the time he dropped her off at the library to pick up her car, he'd become more cautious in his words.

"I can't believe I'm saying this," she told him, "but I really did have a nice time."

"Me, too. You know, Danielle, the Fairmont Farms case doesn't mean we can't be friends."

He saw her hesitation. "Yes, Michael, I think it does."

"Okay, then. We get this over with as soon as possible."

"To you that means Joey goes to his dad, right?" She winked at him. "I think we're back to the bunny slippers."

"Like I said, I've got some moves on this one." He shut her car door for her and left, all the while wondering how a good night kiss would have tasted.

Chapter Three

Temptation Alley. Not a place for a nice girl who had been raised by a cop and a teacher. Not the place nice girls went to look for men. Definitely not the place Danni would pick for a party or to meet a friend. Unfortunately, it was where she now found herself, seated at a back table, incognito.

She fought the urge to remove the coat and scarf she wore to hide her identity. Although the heat threatened to suffocate her, she had to know whether Michael Sommers knew the real deal or blew smoke. The possibility she'd win the case for an unfit

23

mother bothered her more than she wanted to admit.

Various different characters strolled into the bar. More passes than in a Tennessee University football game had come her way. The guy at the next table hadn't taken his eyes off her since she entered. A big guy, he'd asked to buy her a drink earlier, but she'd been able to brush him off with no problem. She still sensed he watched her even though she didn't allow their eyes to meet.

She could barely see them, anyway, because of her dark glasses. But she'd know Mrs. Fairmont if she saw her.

She kept her eyes on the entrance.

That's when the door opened and Michael Sommers stalked through it. She pulled the scarf a little tighter around her and pretended to be studying her drink with an intensity unmerited by the watered-down cola.

Wearing a navy T-shirt and jeans, he walked straight to her table, leaned over her, and hissed, "Let's get out of here."

"Excuse me?"

"You heard me. You don't need to be in

this place, and you certainly don't need to be here alone."

"I can't leave, I'm waiting on someone." It was only half a lie, as that someone just didn't know she waited. "How did you know I was here? Don't tell me intuition. Hugh called you, didn't he?"

"He had a deposition this evening and couldn't stop you himself. Forget him. I knew you'd pull this. It's my fault, though. I shouldn't have told you anything."

"Why would Hugh call *you* of all people?"

"Because you told him what I told you. Which, by the way, I don't appreciate. He reminded me if anything happened to you, it would be my fault."

The waitress who looked too young to be working in a place that sold alcoholic beverages came by and asked Michael what she could get him to drink. He looked at her skimpy outfit and then to Danni. "Nothing, thanks." He pulled money from his pocket and handed it to her. "We're leaving."

"I'm not." Danni couldn't believe this. "I don't know who assigned you my keeper but I've been on my own for years now, and have done just fine, thank you very much. And as for Hugh, he shouldn't have called anyone to baby-sit me." She took off the scarf. The heat, combined with her worked-up state, made the outfit unbearable.

"I won't leave this bar without you. I can't believe you'd come here." Michael's voice began to register anger as he sat down opposite her. "What would you've done if you'd caught her here?"

"What would I have done?" Danni sounded incredulous. But didn't have a real answer.

"That's exactly what I thought, you don't have a clue what to do with the car once you catch it, do you? Now, let's go."

Another man approached them. The one who earlier tried to buy her a drink. Burly, with fur from head to toe, he pointed to Michael, but his eyes were on Danni. "Is this creep bothering you, Honey?"

"No. We know each other." Danni told him to avoid any altercation, "We're just disagreeing on when to leave."

Danni could see Michael size the other

man up. *This could get sticky. I'd better go with Michael.*

"Man of Fur" spoke, "Buddy, the lady can stay if she wants to. But, *you* can go."

"Really?" Sarcasm dripped from Michael's voice. "I appreciate your input, Sasquatch, but she's with me."

Past Michael, Danni saw Sallie Fairmont enter the door.

"Sit down, Michael. Please." No way to motion or tell him what she could see without making a bigger scene.

"You heard the lady," the other man said, "sit down."

"We're leaving." Michael only spoke in concern for her, she knew, but still he spoke through clenched teeth.

"Man of Fur" didn't take it lightly. "Apologize to the lady."

"Apologize?" Michael roared.

Danni's protector disliked it and he proved that when he punched Michael square in the face.

Michael didn't speak to Danni on the way to her house. Since she'd gone to the bar by cab, she allowed him to drive her home. She sat in the passenger seat, as he looked at his left eye in the lighted mirror on the visor.

When they reached her driveway, guilt overwhelmed her. "Would you like a steak for that eye?"

He turned to her. "What I would like to do is return to the bar and finish what that jerk started." If she thought his mood was bad in the bar, it was nothing compared to now. "Unfortunately, I can't do that. And, do you know why?"

His tone left something to be desired, but Michael never raised his voice. "Because we barely got out of there before the bar-tender called the cops." He touched his eye. "Ouch! I wouldn't want anyone to know that I was ever inside Temptation Alley, either."

Once the car was parked, Michael fol-lowed Danni to her front porch. From what he could see in the dark, the house sat on a hill with lots of flowers around its exte-rior. He heard barking from inside.

"Come on in, I'll find you something for your eye."

A pretty brown and black dog jumped on her as she entered the door, walking back-wards on its hind legs to continue being petted even as Danni moved forward into the house.

"Meet Lilly." She continued to pet the dog. "She's my best friend. Well," Danni grinned sheepishly, "other than my sister." She removed her coat and put it on the rack near the door.

Michael sat down on her couch with the realization his eye really did *hurt*. It surprised him when she leaned over him, finger near his eye to study the bruise.

In a softened tone he continued to try and make her see sense. "I just pulled you from the worst place in town. I'd have been plagued with guilt if something happened to you."

"Look, Mike, you didn't have to go there."

"Hugh and I decided—"

"Forget Hugh. You made the decision. I couldn't help that. Or, that the guy with fur liked me."

"How in the world did you get him in a neck hold?"

"I have an older brother."

"Oh. That explains it, but I was winning before you jumped in, you know that."

"That isn't what scared me. The other

guy wasn't doing great, I admit, but I saw the bartender going for 911. If we'd been caught in a brawl—"

"We'd both be ruined." He raised his arms in the air. "Finally, you catch on. Now, where's the steak?"

"I'll just be a moment. Have a seat."

Michael liked the small home where Danni lived. It looked like her—sweet, cheery, and decorated in pretty bright greens and other earth tones. He saw the family portrait above her fireplace. A sister and brother, Danni, and both parents. They looked like a happy family, all smiling for the photo. He wondered if it were a true portrait or like many families, just the picture of what they longed to be. All the while, he absently petted the dog that welcomed Danni home.

She returned from the kitchen with a frozen chicken breast.

He tried, without success, to disguise his annoyance. "You gotta be kidding me."

"Well, I don't eat a lot of red meat. This is all I had in the freezer."

Michael walked over to the foyer and found the mirror over a small table near the door. The dark bruise around his left eye became more visible as he stood there. "I can't go into court looking like this. I can hear it now, 'and, where did you get that shiner, Mr. Sommers? Hanging out at Temptation Alley, again?' "

"That would be good. Then, you wouldn't be lying or anything."

He tried to curb the rekindled anger. "Don't. Just don't." He sat back down on the couch.

"Don't what, Michael? Show up in a bar or save your butt from the big guy?" Beautiful. Frustrating, as all get out, but enticing all the same.

Michael didn't answer her.

She studied him for a moment and then sighed. "Yeah. Luckily for us, Mrs. Fairmont had already found her 'friend' and didn't care about the fight."

Danni sat beside Michael, the cold chicken breast still in her hand. "What should I do with this?"

Michael took it from her and examined it. "I think your dog wants it. Could you round up an ice pack?"

Silently, she returned the chicken to the freezer and got him a plastic bag filled with ice.

He took it from her and held it to his eye. He muttered about going to court and how heinous this would look to the judges and other attorneys. He looked at her from beneath the ice pack. "I don't want to hear that you told anyone about this. If you do I'll . . ." his voice trailed off.

"Sue me?" The sparkle in her chocolate eyes, as attractive as it may have been, just added to his fury.

"This isn't the moment."

"Lighten up, Mike. You've made your point, or should I say *all* your points? I shouldn't have gone to the bar. I shouldn't have beaten that guy up for you. I shouldn't tell anyone what happened. I heard you."

"You didn't beat the guy up. You just broke up the fight."

"As bad as I hate to admit it, you're probably right. Where did *you* learn to fight like that?"

He grinned. "In college. I was known as sort of a smart-alecky kind of guy. I had to learn to shut my mouth or fight."

"Why am I not surprised you chose to fight?"

"I got tired of being afraid."

After a long silence, Danni murmured, "Heroes aren't born, they're made."

Her words dissipated his anger. "So, now I'm a hero?"

"I only mean . . . well, you know."

Still angry, but at least quieted by Danni's speech, Mike could think of nothing else to say. His gaze stayed on her, watching her move about the room as she chatted about the weather and other insignificant matters. Her black hair flowed from a center part, and those laughing dark eyes held him mesmerized.

Her chatter waned. He took the ice bag from his eye. "Danni, come here."

He couldn't hide his surprise when she obeyed.

"Do you need something?" She examined his eye, again.

He sat on the edge of the couch as she stood over him. He took her hand.

Her tone admonished him. "With all your talk of professionalism, this is a clear violation."

He hated to be wrong. But, he knew when to quit. "I'm sorry."

"As well you should be."

"I notice, however, that your hand is still

attached to mine. Would you care to explain that, Miss Price?"

With flustered motions, Danni disentangled herself from him. "Sorry."

He stood and looked down at her. "I'm going to argue Mrs. Fairmont's counsel has dementia."

He followed her to the door and when she opened it, instead of exiting he kissed her cheek. "The only thing that is keeping us apart is this case, right?"

She didn't meet his gaze. "If that's what you want to think, fine. I have no personal feelings in this matter."

He placed a finger beneath her chin, raising her face so their eyes would meet. "If this is your courtroom face, you don't stand a chance."

Her dark eyes sought his. "Michael, I don't want this. Your reputation precedes you and I have no intention of getting involved with you."

"I won't hurt you."

"I'm sure I'm the seven hundred and fifty-first woman to hear that. Good night, Michael."

He sighed. "Good night."

A simple plan formed in his head. Convince Danni he cared and wouldn't hurt her. A hard sale, he admitted to himself. But, he got paid to make the hard sales everyday.

Chapter Four

"What's up, Dad?" Michael answered a summons to his father's office.

His father waved a hand, gesturing for Michael to close the door. "Do you remember two years ago when I took Pete Randall for a mint in divorce court?"

"Oh, yeah." Michael grinned, remembering the victory party well. "He loved you for that. You should think twice when working against a local news producer."

"I got this note from him today." He read it aloud. "Jason, glad to see you did your job well. Maybe you should stay with divorces where you can stick it to your opponents. Your friend always, Pete Randall.' " He held up a videotape case and told Michael, "He sent me this tape of the news clippings from the Dogwood Manor case."

The television came on when Jason hit the remote buttons, the VCR followed suit.

The reporter on the scene, a gentleman in his mid-thirties wearing a suit, stood with a smiling Danni Price. "Miss Price, are you happy to have won such an important case?"

"It has been an honor to represent Judy Dorsey. As you know, her family has owned the Dogwood Manor for generations."

"But," the reporter asked, "you have to take pleasure in knowing that you've been an attorney for less than two years, and your opposing counsel was Jason Sommers?"

Michael saw Danni pause. "Mr. Sommers did his job well, as he always does. In all my dealings with him on this case, he has been the perfect gentleman and jurist. I can only say the verdict came from a jury who happened to agree with my client's position."

"Can you elaborate on that?" The reporter asked her.

"Dogwood Manor is a home and soon to be a bed and breakfast that will not only be a family business but a landmark for Fort White. This is more important than the industrial area that the county wanted to make it."

"Miss Price, do you believe that the plans you presented in court will be used by the county?"

"Let's hope so. Putting an industrial park in a residential area is just not what these people wanted. The jury heard the evidence and agreed. Thank you."

Danni walked away, leaving the reporter to talk with her client.

Jason flipped the VCR and the television off. "You know, when Carl Johnson and I walked out of there, people were actually yelling 'home stealer' at us." Jason offered Michael a soda and continued, "It's strange. She looks like such a sweet young thing. Who'd have thought?"

"Hey," Michael pointed out, "at least she said nice things about you." He quoted her: "You're the perfect gentleman and jurist."

Jason snorted. "How dare she be gracious?"

"Have you filed the appeal?"

"Didn't you hear her? She not only beat me, she found another site, for sale I may add, that the county government is going to look at for the industrial park. I need an aspirin."

Michael walked into the half bath off his dad's office and came back with the medicine bottle. "She really outdid herself for a first-timer."

"I did the unthinkable, Mike. I underestimated my opponent. She's bright, enthusiastic. As bad as I hate to say it, I think we need to be more careful in cases against her. And, don't forget this in the Fairmont case. I know you took her out for the auction, but . . ." His dad hesitated. "Is there something wrong with your eye?"

"Uh, no. I leaned over to pick up my toothbrush and cracked my head on the sink."

He walked to Michael to examine it closer. "Is it covered in make-up?"

"Yeah, I hit it hard. Stopped this morning and found something to hide it."

"That's quite a shiner for a sink to make. It looks more like someone hit you."

"Yeah, I know. Hurt like hell. Didn't want people thinking I'd been hanging out at Temptation Alley."

Jason chuckled. "I'd like to see you in there. You'd probably come out looking like that."

Inwardly, Michael groaned. "You're probably right."

"As I was saying, don't underestimate that gal."

"I won't, Dad. I appreciate the head's up."

Danni's workload evolved after winning the Dogwood Manor case. No longer did she do simple bankruptcies, uncontested divorces, and briefs for the other attorneys. She didn't even get the chance for lunch some days, now that her employers realized she could actually practice law.

She welcomed the work. It helped her to forget Michael's visit to her house. His touch still made her hand and cheek tingle.

The folder Danni picked up held notice of Mr. Fairmont's intention to fight for custody in his answer and cross-complaint.

That meant more time with Michael and to wonder if she were doing the right thing by even representing Sallie.

"Danni?" Hugh strolled into her office, smiling like a Cheshire cat. "You looked like you were somewhere else for a moment."

"No. I'm right here." Okay, so it was a barefaced lie. She'd been at home, holding hands with Michael Sommers. So what? Whose business was it what she dreamed?

"I have something that will make you very happy."

She sighed. "I am very happy, Hugh."

He eyed her, disbelief on his face. "All right, then." He sat on the corner of her desk. "I have something that will make you *happier*."

"Okay, I'll bite. What do you have to make me happier than I am right now?"

"Tickets to Don Giovanni, given to me by a happy client. I know how you love opera, so I'm asking you to go with me."

Danni did feel better upon hearing the news. "Hugh, how incredible. That performance has been sold out for weeks. What do you say I cook?"

"No. Dinner is on me, because I couldn't

get you out of that auction like we planned."

"But, Hugh—"

He waved a hand in dismissal of anything she had to say. "No, Danni. It's not like it will be an expensive evening. We'll eat and go to the opera on me. That's final."

"Okay. I'll bring my dress to work with me, and we can leave from here."

"Oh, and Danni," Hugh smiled. "Pete Randall at the news station sent over a copy of your interview on the Dogwood Manor case. Greene has it. He's ecstatic."

She knew she beamed. "Really? Mr. Greene showed emotion?"

"Unusual, huh? The bad news is you'd better watch Mike Sommers on your Fairmont case." His smile faded. "This will mean revenge."

The ground fell out from beneath her. "I'm sure you're right. Thanks, Hugh."

Danni looked over the papers in the folder. *Michael Sommers is any other attorney. The Fairmont divorce is any other case.* Her mantra continued for as long as she looked over the file.

Chapter Five

The Tennessee Theater, full to capacity with opera fans, echoed the high spirits of the occasion. A seasoned veteran who always turned out marvelous performances played the lead. Michael knew they wouldn't be disappointed. His date, Sharon, a pretty lady with copper hair, long legs, and a figure that men watched, loved opera second-to-none. She also had no sign of being more than a friend and had announced her engagement a few weeks ago. When she called to say she had come to town on business, they decided to get together tonight for the show.

Last night, he'd received a call from his mother, wanting to set him up with a friend's daughter and two calls from a girl he'd taken out once, a month ago. It made him glad to share an evening with someone who didn't cling or expect more from him than he wanted to give, at least for the moment.

Not only that, he admitted only to himself he needed a break from the emotions Danni Price evoked in him.

Sharon's friend status made her a breath of fresh air.

He took her hand to lead her to their seats when he spotted Danni. Why did his heart begin to race at the very sight of her? Could it be she looked like some kind of goddess in a dress that looked black but shimmered with violet highlights?

She'd seen him.

Danni couldn't believe getting away from Michael would be so hard. But there he stood, dressed in a black tuxedo, and with a gorgeous redhead on his arm. She'd been right to turn him away.

Okay, so she was right. Obviously he rebounded quite nicely to her rejection. *No one could look as good as that woman. In fact, no one should. It should be . . . illegal.*

She wrapped both arms around Hugh's and whispered to him, "There's Mike Sommers."

"I didn't peg him for an opera buff."

"Look at the woman with him. I'll bet that hair color isn't natural."

She left herself defenseless to Hugh's sidelong glance and observation. "Is that the green-eyed monster I hear?"

Danni apologized, realizing how her words sounded. "I can't believe I said that."

Hugh turned his head to face her. "Danni, you aren't the first woman to fall under his spell."

"I'm sure I won't be the last, either." She kissed Hugh on the cheek. "I'm glad you're here."

"Me, too. Just remember something my grandmother told me."

"Which is?"

"A leopard can't change his spots."

Michael would always be a man women sought after and probably never settle down. Not at all what Danni wanted from life.

"Your grandmother must have been a wise woman."

Hugh led Danni through the crowd. "Oh, I don't know about that. It took her three marriages to realize it. She wanted me to be an attorney to save her legal fees."

Danni chuckled. "I've never met anyone who can ruin a good story like you can. Oh, no. Here they come. Smile."

"I *am* smiling."

Michael, too, looked as if someone had plastered an unnatural grin on his face. "Hey, Danni, Hugh. It's nice to see you both."

Hugh shook Michael's offered hand. "I didn't know you liked opera, Mike."

"Oh, yeah. Season tickets. This is Sharon Garrett. We went to law school together at Tennessee University."

Danni offered Sharon her hand and as she shook it Sharon sang Danni's praises. "I'm in Nashville, now, but your Dogwood Manor case made the rounds even there. Congratulations."

"Thank you." Did she have to be so nice? Danni really wanted to hate her. "It's a tough fight when you know your opponent is the best attorney in town." She secretly hoped Michael heard her comment and would be appreciative.

Sharon shared her opinion. "That *does* have a psychological impact going into the courtroom."

Hugh asked Sharon a question about a judge in Nashville, and Danni faced Michael with a plastic smile.

He whispered to her, "You look wonderful tonight."

Her smile became genuine. "You look pretty dapper yourself."

"We need to get together."

She hadn't expected that, not with Sharon standing two feet away. "Excuse me?"

"On the Fairmonts. Call me next week."

Hugh saved Danni from more small talk. "We really should take our seats. Nice meeting you, Sharon."

"You too." *Why did the woman's smile have to be so sincere and beautiful?* Danni wanted to be sick.

They parted ways then, each couple going towards their own seats.

Hugh's tickets were first row balcony, which was fine because Danni brought her opera glasses, and the seats gave them a terrific view. One of her favorite places in all of Fort White, she studied the theater's beautiful ornate auditorium.

Looking through the glasses she focused first on the stage, then on the beautiful carved walls. Next, however, she found Michael. He and the redhead were just a few rows ahead of them, but on the first floor.

They talked. He smiled at her a lot. They laughed.

Danni became incensed. He enjoyed himself with this woman, the cad. How could he do that after asking her out? She leaned forward for a better view. The person on her left bumped her arm and the small binoculars sailed out of her hands and into the seats below.

Oh, no! Danni sat back, trying to hide herself from anyone's view. But, she saw where they landed, right in Michael's lap. *This can't be happening.*

Because no one paid attention to her moves, the crowd was unable to locate the seat from which the glasses fell. To avoid being spotted, she became involved in the conversation behind her, something about a singer whose voice failed him during an important performance. *Safe.* No one noticed. No reason to be embarrassed. All's well.

Hugh, who'd been visiting a few rows away, sat down next to her as the lights dimmed.

Several minutes passed when he asked to borrow her glasses.

"Oh," she thought a moment, "I can't find them."

"You must have left them in the car. Too bad, I'd love to have had them tonight."

Later, on the way out of the theater, they once again ran into Michael and his date.

Danni smiled sweetly and attempted to define the relationship between the couple. "Did you enjoy yourselves?"

Sharon dried her eyes. "It was wonderful. I love Don Ottavio's aria of his love for Dona Anna."

Danni's favorite, as well. "I know. The tenor sang beautifully."

Hugh offered to go get his car and Sharon offered to keep Danielle company until he returned.

With unease, Danni tried to concentrate on the small talk Sharon made. She answered and nodded at what she hoped were the appropriate intervals. Finally, she told them, "You have no reason to stay with me. I'm fine and Hugh will be here any minute."

"Why don't you join us for a late dinner?" Sharon asked.

"Oh, we ate before the show. But, thank you. Don't let me keep you from your own supper. You must be starved."

"I *am* starting to look at Mike's tie and wonder how it would taste with a little salt."

Michael faltered. "If you're sure you'll be all right, I'll take Sharon to dinner, then."

"I'm fine. Really. Hugh will return any time, now."

Michael smiled as Sharon said her good-byes. Danni watched as they walked away. The crowd had dissipated and she had a clear shot of the pair as they left. She acknowledged them as a striking couple.

That's when Michael pulled something from his pocket and threw it over his shoulder. Danni caught her opera glasses like a pro football player.

Oh, no. He knew. She sighed. She'd

never live it down. No one else appeared to see his actions, or hers. *Thank God.*

Looking back on the situation: The auction no longer held the gold medal as Danni's most embarrassing moment.

"Your Honor, a child of six needs his mother. It's not customary to give the father full custody. I know Mr. Fairmont has more money. In many families, the father *is* the major breadwinner. But, with his proper support, there is no reason Mrs. Fairmont can not take care of her child."

"Your Honor—" Michael stopped at the Judge's interruption.

"Mr. Sommers, unless you can present this court with evidence to the contrary, I happen to agree with Miss Price."

"My client contends that Mrs. Fairmont is not fit for the custody of his child, your Honor."

Judge Marcus Miller sat back in his chair, his hand ready at the gavel as murmurings in the courtroom swelled then died down. Known as a just man, but a hard judge, his look alone gave the room reason to quiet.

Danni played her card. "This is ridiculous, Your Honor. We all know this is another wealthy man who believes everything should come easy to him."

Judge Miller, a man in his sixties with graying hair did not appear impressed with Michael's reasons. "Mr. Sommers, we all know this divorce is news and false allegations to get custody of the child could slander Mrs. Fairmont. Can you give me solid proof that the child is in danger?"

"No, Your Honor, but—"

"No buts, Counselor. I award temporary custody to the mother, with weekend visitation and the usual twenty-one percent income as support." He hit the gavel to the desk. His gaze fell to Michael. "As for you. I want something in thirty days. And let me warn you, Mr. Sommers, it had better be solid and leave me no doubt. Have I made myself clear?"

"Yes. Crystal clear."

Danni spoke. "If I may, Your Honor. Perhaps this could all be worked out without bringing the child to court."

"Excellent idea, Miss Price. I'm sure the Fairmonts are paying you both enough to keep it civil." The Judge's slam of the gavel dismissed them.

Michael caught Danni in the hall. "My dad was right about you. Bright, enthusiastic. I'm just surprised you didn't back me up in there."

"I had to make a decision over the last week. I'm an attorney, not a social worker. I'm here to represent Sallie Fairmont and that's what I intend to do." She hesitated. "I believe that Sallie may have her faults, but I know she loves her little boy and won't do anything to put him in danger. That's what this is all about." *Make his scent go away. Don't let me be taken in by his charm and good looks. Make me see reason to all of this.*

"You know, Danni. If you were another attorney, I'd probably argue the point with you. But, at this stage of law for you, that's the right choice. That is, if you plan on staying in law."

She hoped she looked stern. "That's the plan."

"Let me check my calendar and get back with you on scheduling, okay?"

"We're ready to go anytime."

He turned to leave, then turned back to her. "By the way, what are you doing for dinner tomorrow night?"

She stepped close to him so no one else could hear her. "I'm going to Temptation Alley. Since your eye is nearly well, you want to go another round?"

Though he grinned, he said, "I wish that were funny."

"I've noticed you've been able to keep it mostly covered."

"Yes, I've lied to everyone though. I told them I leaned over and hit it on the bathroom sink."

"A little white lie and not malicious."

"I've also learned the finer points of the uses of make-up foundation."

"Having a hobby makes us all well-rounded."

Michael looked away from her a moment, still grinning, and then back to her. "This is still all your fault."

"I knew that was coming."

"I'll let you cook tomorrow night and make it up to me. And, I'll do you another favor. I won't put a letter to the editor in the News Journal saying I want to return a pair of opera glasses."

The heat in Danni's face told her what color her skin must be. "They've been returned, safe and sound." She looked at the floor a minute. "Won't Sharon mind if we have dinner?" She looked back to Michael to see his expression.

It didn't change. "No. She won't."

"Still, I think it best for us to stay on a professional level."

Michael picked up the briefcase he'd sat on the floor when they met in the hall. "Should've held the opera glasses hostage."

No other words would suffice. She stood motionless as he left.

Chapter Six

Michael smiled all the way back to his office. Danni had slipped up and didn't even know it. She let him know she was jealous. Of Sharon, of all people. Yes, beautiful, but an old friend who had her own fiancé.

This is great. She must have feelings or she wouldn't have said those things.

Oh, no. She had feelings for him. He walked into his office, threw his jacket over the chair and stood behind his desk, leaning both hands on it. "How do I feel about this?"

"About what?"

"Oh, Dad." Mike straightened upon his father's entrance. "I just got back from court."

"Then, I hope you're feeling the thrill of victory."

"Not really. We're going to try to keep the Fairmonts out of court, which is the move I wanted. But, she got temporary custody."

"I told you to watch that Price girl. She's got a spark."

Michael rolled his eyes and sat down. "Tell me about it."

His father considered him. "I hope you don't have a thing for this gal, because she'll wear you out in court if she knows it."

"Don't worry. She isn't going to beat me on this."

"I hope not. She's not someone I'd like to see you get involved with, anyway." Jason sat down across from Michael.

"I always thought business was business. Where is *this* coming from?"

"A beautiful woman can sway a man. If she's not on staff here, she's—more or less—the enemy. I don't like it, but this case is solid proof of my philosophy."

"In other words, this case keeps us at odds with each other."

"In my opinion, not just this case, but the fact that she works for the other large firm in town. She's the competition, Mike."

His dad stood. "I hope I didn't burst any bubbles for you." On that note his father left him alone in his office.

Michael didn't want to explain to his father his regard for Danielle Price. Nothing stood in his way with her except the Fairmont case, which could be settled post haste. He knew Danni would understand it was only business when he won.

Wait. Cramer called him when she went on her merry way to Temptation Alley. He escorted her to the opera, and the night of the auction, he bid on her.

Michael took a deep breath. The auction had been two weeks ago today. In that time, he couldn't stop thinking about her. Now, he realized however, that Hugh Cramer probably played a bigger role in the picture than he'd first thought.

He had to find out. Who did he know over at Greene and Smelcer? The phone buzzed, breaking into his reverie.

"Yes?"

"Michael, Mr. Cramer is on line three for you."

Speak of the devil.

"Thanks." He picked up the phone. "Michael Sommers."

"Michael, Hugh Cramer, here. Did you send over that final settlement on the Crown Hardware accident?"

Some poor schmuck had pulled on a piece of pipe and the whole display had come tumbling down atop him.

"I think so. Maybe Danni has it. We've corresponded a lot lately on the Fairmont case. It might have gotten put in with her mail." Maybe Hugh would let something slip.

Cramer hesitated. "I'll ask her."

"I hope if it is, it's not a problem. I assume you see Danni every day." Mike would get to the bottom of the story with that comment.

"No problem, at all. I'll check with the secretary." Hugh hung up the phone as Danni strode into his office.

"Want to tell me the joke?" Danni asked him. "I could use the laugh."

Hugh grinned. "Somebody likes you."

"Me? Really? Is it that guy who works

at circuit court? You know the one who's young enough to nap on a mat and always has a stupid grin on his face whenever a female enters the room?"

Hugh drew the word out, "No-oo."

Danni pulled a book from the shelf and looked back at Hugh. "You're serious, aren't you?"

He nodded. "Big time."

She pushed him on the shoulder. "Then tell me!"

Hugh's brow arched in mischief. "Let's just say, someone just acted very strange about us working together."

Danni couldn't contain her curiosity. "Us? As in you and me?"

He nodded. "Yep."

She sat down in the chair across from his desk. "What did you tell him?"

Hugh didn't give anything away. "Nothing. He's a smart guy, let him put the puzzle together."

She looked for a way to drag the information from her friend. "I could use a good dinner. Who's the guy?"

"To be honest, I don't think you'll believe me."

She reached across the desk and took his

hand. "If you don't tell me after you've piqued my interest, I will sue you for breach of promise." She not only dropped his hand, but slapped it as well. "Now, who's the mystery man?"

Hugh's teasing laughter affected her and she chuckled with him. "Come on, Hugh, spill it."

"Mike Sommers."

Danni's laughter died. "Why in the world would you think he likes *me*?"

"Because as nonchalant as he may try to be, he's asking about *us*." Hugh sat back in his seat. "You know, now that I think about it, he flew to your rescue at the bar. He couldn't keep his eyes off you when we met him at the opera. He must really be attracted, Danni."

She didn't know how she should answer him. She didn't want to discuss Michael Sommers with Hugh, or anyone else for that matter. Her cheek still felt warm from his kiss the night of the "bar incident."

"Are you still with me?" Hugh's voice cut into her thoughts.

"Sure. It's not like there's any meat to go with those potatoes. I'm not involved with him. I don't expect to be. There's no way I'd go out with him."

Hugh stared hard at Danni for a long moment. "I'm concerned. A moment ago this was all a joke."

"There isn't anything to be worried about, Hugh. I have it all under control."

As she got up and tugged on the hem of her suit jacket, Hugh also stood, touching her arm to keep her from leaving the room. "I took you under my wing from day one."

Danni couldn't meet his eyes. "I know that."

"Listen, *your* feelings are the important thing."

She looked at him. "You want to know if I'm falling for the opposing counsel in one of the most important cases we have on the books right now."

He looked solemn. "Are you?"

She sat back down. She didn't want to lie to him. He'd always been so good to her. "Hugh, Mike Sommers is a nice guy. He's smart and handsome and charming."

"But?"

She sighed. "He opposes us in court and has a reputation for women."

"You know, Teresa Daniels is the Assistant D.A. and her husband is a criminal lawyer. It wouldn't be the first time this has happened, Danni."

"Ah, yes." She raised a finger to make her point. "But, before they married was he known for his escapades with women? Michael Sommers is his own worst enemy. Because he's got those big blue come-and-get-me eyes, the women can't help themselves. He has them whether he wants them or not."

Hugh smirked. "Mike Sommers is like Billy the Kidd."

"Which means, what?"

"His reputation is highly exaggerated. Yeah, he's had his share, but no one has that many women, not even him."

She didn't pretend hope in this matter. "He has no commitment. He knows that if I say no, there will be five more ready to take my place."

Hugh didn't give up his viewpoint. "True, but isn't that your decision to make before he moves on?"

"In answer to your question, Hugh, I don't want to be involved with Michael Sommers. Feel better?"

He eyed her a long moment. "Not really."

She groaned as she left his office carrying a book she needed for family court. Of course, now that she had the information, all she could do was think about Mike.

He'd actually had the audacity to ask Hugh about her. She should be mad, but instead she wanted to pick up the phone and tell her sister, Tess, that she had a man in her life. She didn't really *have* a man in her life. But, she could have.

If she wanted one.

But, she didn't.

Danni sat in Michael's office across from him in a chair more comfortable than her own office chair. Michael, who sat reading the documents she'd brought with her, looked as if he were appalled.

He didn't speak, but as he studied the forms he would occasionally huff and puff, like the big, bad wolf in the fairy tale. Only to irritate Danni more, Michael muttered.

She could take it no longer. "There is nothing wrong with this settlement. Everything in it is fair."

He threw the papers down on the large

oak desk in front of him, loosening his tie as he spoke. "Sure it is, if your name happens to be Sallie Fairmont. I can't go back to Joe with this. In fact, let me make it even more clear to you. I *won't* go back to him. Not as-is."

Danni did some puffing of her own. "She didn't ask for the family estate."

Annoyance flickered in his voice. "You've got enough alimony in here to buy Mexico."

The two had been at it for almost an hour trying to settle the Fairmont case before court. "If you would just listen to yourself. This woman has every right to the same lifestyle she had with him."

He shook his head and pushed his finger against the papers in front of him. "No. Just because the big guy has money, that doesn't mean that she should get it all. She didn't earn it. She married into it."

Danni became incensed. "And, that's her fault? Besides, he was born into it. Does that mean he shouldn't have it, either?"

"He wasn't born for money, she married it on purpose."

"He's the one who wants the divorce. Irreconcilable differences. There's no hint that she's done anything wrong."

"You know—"

"It doesn't matter what I know, Mike. You, of all people, should understand that. What matters is my client's welfare. That's why I'm here." Danni took time out to look at her watch. "I'm starved."

Michael stretched and covered a yawn. "Okay, let's finish this over dinner."

"Sounds good." She picked up her purse. Why shouldn't they eat together? Business sometimes required meetings with food. Lunch meetings. Brunch meetings. Breakfast meetings. Why not a dinner meeting?

"Great. Let me get my jacket." He put it on and they left his office for a little coffee shop downtown, as it was too late for much else.

The shop was crowded for almost nine o'clock.

Michael ushered her to a table near the side door. "We should have never planned this summit so late."

"I know," she agreed, "but I've been in court for the past two days."

She sat down as he pulled her chair out

for her. "Big case?" He sat down opposite her.

The waitress came by and they both ordered burgers and fries.

When she left them alone, Danni answered him. "No. Two cases. One a divorce that I still think the guy should have gotten everything and left that . . . witch with just the clothes on her back."

He chuckled. "I know who *you* represented."

"You'd be wrong. I was *her* counsel."

He put his water glass down without taking a drink "Good going, Danni. Finally getting the hang of it. Not who you like but what your job is."

"Another case today, though, I lost big time. *That* one, I should have won."

He leaned his chin on his hand, arm resting on the table. "So, what have you learned, Dorothy?"

"The *Wizard of Oz*, my favorite." His humor became a warm enchantment around her. "I learned that if I go hunting for happiness, to remember that justice is blind and sometimes it doesn't matter who is right or wrong, all that matters is what a jury or judge believes."

"Does right or wrong matter?" He picked up his water glass and took a sip, waiting for her answer.

"I think I want to be very careful of the cases I take in the future. Plus, I don't believe I want to go into criminal law."

He nodded. "I tried a criminal case once. I swore I'd stick to corporate law after the thief I got off one day was back in jail within two weeks."

Their soft drinks arrived at the table.

"If I could, I'd set myself up to do nothing but pro-bono work for the indigent and battered women."

He took her hand, across the table and held it. "Quite noble pursuits. Especially for someone with your talent."

"Which means?" She didn't draw her hand away, instead she allowed the simple caress of his thumb across her knuckles. The tingling feeling from the night of Temptation Alley returned. She didn't realize until that moment that she'd missed it.

"That you are a brilliant young attorney whose talent will take you far."

She could only nod. It wasn't really an

agreement, but it was all she could do at that moment.

His voice became a mere whisper. "What I really want, Danni, is to talk about us."

She, too, whispered. "I think that we are—oh-my-gosh, don't turn around."

"Why not?"

She tried not to look over his shoulder. "Because Joe Fairmont is over in the corner with that blonde newscaster from Channel Seven."

The mood shattered when Michael withdrew his hand. "That's not funny."

"Am I laughing?"

She saw Michael turn his head to the left. "Don't turn around." She reiterated and smirked. "How dare he want you to go after Sallie? One is as bad as the other. Look at them all over each other, no, don't turn around."

He followed her orders, but she knew he didn't like the situation. "You could be mistaken."

She lowered her voice, her tone thread with insistence. "I saw him just the other day in court. I know the man when I see him."

He drawled with distinct irritation. "I wish I could see for myself."

"Actually, we should move, or leave."

He leaned forward on the table. "Oh?"

"How would you feel with what we're getting paid, if you saw the attorneys on your case at dinner together?"

He considered that thought a moment, then nodded. "You're right."

"I'll get the food to go. Meet me at the car in a few minutes. When you leave, take the side door."

"I don't think—"

"I'm good at this. You'll just have to trust me."

He put the money for the food on the table. "Good grief, Danni, how much experience have you had sneaking out of restaurants?"

"We'll discuss that later."

Danni squashed an urge to let Mr. Fairmont see her. But, good sense overcame the desire. For once.

She got the food and met Michael at the car.

Back at his office, they ate in silence.

She supposed Mike was embarrassed by

the situation, as she had been when Sallie's true colors were exposed.

But, the truth hit her hard. She didn't want to talk about Sallie Fairmont and Temptation Alley. She hated to speak of what they'd, or should she say, she'd just seen?

All she wanted was time to contemplate the man in front of her. His cologne, a woodsy smell. His eyes blue, intelligent, clear. But, regardless of those things, the air of pure self-confidence he exuded caught Danni more.

She tried harder to concentrate on her burger, which was pretty good when one thought about it.

As if that were her thoughts.

"You know what this means?" Danni finally said.

Michael wiped his mouth with his napkin. "It means that it doesn't matter where the child is, it's all the same."

"That's exactly what it means." Danni closed the paper over a small portion of leftover burger. "You know, we could drag this out and make that much more money. But, I just don't work that way. We don't need to know more. We've both got the picture. Settle with us. Show us some money and we'll be done."

"Once we *are* done, can you and I make a fresh start?"

She didn't want to lie to him. "Probably not."

She knew from his nod, he wouldn't ask again. "Let me see what I can do."

Chapter Seven

"**J**oe, I know Joey means a lot to you—"

Joe Fairmont pushed a pudgy finger onto Michael's desk. "He's the center of it all. I want him, Mike. I want him in my home. I don't want to have to ask *her* for him. I don't want her to have a say over when I can and can't have him."

Mike pursed his lips. This would be the hardest sale of his career. "You *don't* want to go to court."

His response held a note of impatience. "I'm not afraid of that tramp!"

Michael sat at his desk with Joe across from him. "I don't suppose you are. But, I doubt Sallie's attorney will leave the court-house without a decent settlement."

His client became more irritated. "Sallie gets *nothing*. Miss Price doesn't even know about Sallie's undying devotion to Temp-tation Alley."

"None of that matters. You have nothing that indicates she endangers Joey. There is no physical danger. There are no grounds to make you appear a better parent than Mrs. Fairmont. The judge is only going to think of physical danger, that's all." He wanted to say he was no better than his wife, but that wouldn't help anything.

"Maybe I should have Danielle Price to represent me."

No time to be hurt. Cole, Sommers and Sommers had been on retainer with Fair-mont Farms for longer than Mike had been in law. The companies were family traditions for each other. "You don't mean that, Joe. You know we always get the job done."

"Not this time. I'm serious, Mike. Old friends or not, Joey is *mine*. If you can't get him for me, I'll find someone who can."

"All right. Then, we go to court. We

serve notice that our stance is she's unfit."

Michael saw relief in Joe's eyes. "She never spends any time with him. She leaves him alone, sometimes. I know you can make this work, Mike. I know it."

Even if Joe had a mistress, this was a new twist for the story. "I didn't realize she left him alone. We can make that work for us."

Appeased, Joe asked, "Can we do something legal that could get him away from her now? I really need him on the sixth."

Michael looked up from his writing. "The sixth? Is it for a family gathering or something?"

"We're shooting a commercial. I need him there."

For some reason, Michael became uneasy. He stood and took his jacket off, walking to the rack near his door and hanging it up. "You don't believe she'll allow him to come as long as she has custody?"

Joe snorted. "Of course not. What do you think this is about? She's just using him against me."

How many times did custody cases come down to that? The children held as hostage for every little whim.

"Let me contact Miss Price. There may be something we can do."

Joe stood and shook Mike's hand. "I appreciate it, Mike. I hated to appear heavy-handed, but I have all the reasons in the world to want Joey with me."

"I'll do what I can, Joe, but you need to understand the judge—"

"Don't worry about him, just work to get Joey to me by the sixth, even if it's a forty-eight hour visitation."

Joe left, nodding to Michael but without saying another word.

Two weeks. He had two weeks to find a way to get a court date and convince a judge that Joe should have custody of his son.

Maybe this wouldn't be so bad if something didn't feel so wrong. He had a constant niggling in the back of his mind that something didn't click, as it should. Once again, he went over the divorce papers. All seemed in order.

As opposing counsel he saw Danielle B. Price at the bottom of the form. He needed to make a call.

He picked up his phone. "Carol, get Danni Price on the phone, would you?"

In a moment, Carol buzzed him back. "Miss Price on line four, Michael."

He reached for the phone. "Danni, it's Mike."

"What's up?"

"I'm not sure. I wondered, could we get together for a few minutes today?

He could hear pages turning in the background. He assumed she checked her calendar as he waited. "When did you have in mind?"

"Either one-thirty or four would be good for me."

"I'll be there right after lunch, then."

"You've talked with Sallie Fairmont this week?" Michael's words were all business, even if his mind thought that Danni looked too good in business clothes.

"Yes. We're taking a hard line, too."

Michael nodded. "We're doing the same." He paused for a long moment, letting himself drift in her soft brown eyes. "Danni, is everything all right with this case? I keep reading the documentation and can't find anything wrong, but still I feel as if something isn't . . . there. I sound like an idiot."

Danni opened her briefcase, laying forms on the desk between them. "It's funny you should say that. I get the same impression. Like you, I've read and reread." As if to prove her point she picked up the papers and studied them. He pretended to do the same, but he really couldn't concentrate. She wore flowery perfume that made his pulse race a little faster than usual.

"Any suggestions?" Michael had a few. They had nothing to do with the case, but everyone was allowed their own thoughts, right?

"I've come to one conclusion, Michael. I think we need to get them together and meet the boy. Maybe when we get all the pigs in the pen, as my grandma used to say, we'll have a better idea of how we should handle it."

"That may be the only way to go." The time was appropriate to look at her and he stole the moment to do so.

"From what we've seen," she continued, "it isn't as if one parent is more qualified than the other."

Mike couldn't help but be sarcastic. "That's for sure. On the other hand, can you arrange a visit for Joe?"

"He already has him every weekend."

"Joe wants a forty-eight hour visit on the sixth. He's shooting a Fairmont Farms commercial and wants Joey there. Can you check with Sallie and see what she wants?"

"I'll do my best. But, I can't promise." Danni stood. As a courtesy, so did Michael. He realized that she would be the perfect height to put his arm around her shoulders. Her silky voice glided over him. "I'd say the best way to Sallie's heart is *his* pocketbook. You want Joey for a few days? Simply have Joe offer to send her on a vacation to 'ease her nerves' while her baby is away from her." Danni shook her head and he sensed an odd twinge of disappointment. "You know, when Greene gave me this case, I thought I'd arrived. Now, I feel like my train never left the station."

"The trains we think aren't running can be the ones that go the furthest."

"I thought you practiced law. I didn't know you were also a philosopher."

"In our line of work, we're a little bit of everything."

For a long moment, they stood just looking into each other's eyes.

It was Danni who finally spoke. "Thanks for the encouragement."

Michael changed the subject. "You want to go for a drink after work?"

She looked away and moved toward the door. She thought the last time he wouldn't ask again. She now knew he'd not give up without a fight. "Not while we're on this case, Mike. It makes me too uncomfortable."

"Okay, but once this case is over—"

She paused, her hand on the doorknob. "There will probably be another one."

He pursed his lips in resignation. "Let me know about the visit, will you?"

"First, find out where he's willing to send her on holiday. Then, I'll try to work it out."

Chapter Eight

"I shouldn't have eaten so much. I'll never get all those papers graded." Tess Price, the family blond, addressed the entire table, but Danni noted the look of blame she gave their mother.

Claudette eyed her daughter as if she were ten and in need of grounding. "You knew what Sunday lunch would be like when you walked through the door. Which means you are also aware of the fact that you'll help me clean up whether you ate too much or not."

"Yes, Mother." All three of the Price children chided their mom.

The family, close-knit from the womb, always worked to have as many Sunday dinners at home as they could. The house where they grew up had only recently been remodeled and Danni felt a little off-kilter as the kitchen now had a dishwasher and other conveniences she wasn't used to having at her parents' home.

Her pager sounded, and she excused herself to her old bedroom. The one she'd shared with her younger sister until she got through college and out on her own.

When she checked it, she knew the number. "Michael Sommers."

"Who's that?" Tess asked from behind her.

Helpless to halt her discomfort, she hoped Tess didn't notice. "An attorney. We're opposing counsel on a case."

Tess stood in front of her without an offer to leave so Danni could make her call.

"Tess, do you mind?"

She grinned mischievously. "Not usually."

"I'd like to make my call."

"I'm your sister. Why would you want me out of the room to make a call? Is this some kind of big secret thing you're working on?"

"My business is always confidential." Did Danni really think she could slip something past Tess?

"Um, yeah. You look more like you're anxious to talk with this *guy*. So, tell me about him."

She sighed. "After the call, okay?"

"Okay. I'll be in the den, waiting for a full report."

"You sound like a teacher."

"I am a teacher."

"Then," Danni said as she dialed, "I guess it's good you sound like one."

Tess left the room as the number rang.

The voice that met her ears was all business. "Mike Sommers."

"Hi. It's me."

She could hear his face break into a smile even on the phone. "Well, hello, me. How you doing?"

"Fine."

"Where are you?"

"Family Sunday lunch. You paged me?"

"I wanted to talk to you." After the thought, he didn't say anything else.

"About the case?"

"Of course. I wouldn't dare break Danielle B. Price's rules of engagement. After all, we *are* working on a case. So, you got a few minutes later today?"

After a brief hesitation, she answered him, "That might be a good idea. We need to sort some things through."

He sounded excited. "Good."

"My house at six o'clock. And, Michael, I was raised by a teacher. I don't tolerate tardiness."

"Yes, ma'am. Six o'clock."

Danni hung up the phone before she embarrassed herself more. She needed to talk and luckily, Tess was downstairs waiting on her.

Tess sat on the couch reading a magazine when Danni entered the den. "The dishwasher is the most wonderful invention. A woman obviously holds the patent."

Danni sat down next to her sister. "That's a statement I'll agree with."

Tess put the magazine down. "You're killing me with curiosity, who's this guy?"

"The man I'm in love with."

Tess's eyes grew as big as saucers. "Then talk, sister."

"He's a third generation attorney. Never

had to work a real day in his life, probably. Tall, dark hair, and eyes so blue I feel like I'm drowning when he looks at me."

"God, Danni. When did all this happen?"

"Oh, going on three weeks ago, now. He's the guy I told you about that bought the dinner at the auction."

Confusion clouded Tess's pretty face. "Wait a minute. You hate that guy."

"I know. And, I'm also in love with him. You know math, add two plus two."

Tess lay back against a pillow on the couch. "How does he feel?"

"About the same as I do."

Tess took a moment to think before she questioned Danni further. "Let me get all this straight. This guy is tall."

Danni nodded. "I'd say six-three."

"Handsome?"

"More like drop dead gorgeous."

"And, single?"

"Of course!" Danni retorted. As if she'd go out with a married man.

"You're in love with him, and you think he feels the same way?"

"Yep."

"Tell me, again, why this is such a bad thing, Danni. Because somewhere along the line, I'm missing the point of this discussion."

"He's the opposing counsel in the biggest case of my career."

"But, not forever. Right? I mean, after the case is closed you can get together."

"You don't know this guy's reputation. He abhors commitment. He'll bolt once I make a move."

"And break your heart."

Danni looked away, not daring to face her sister at that moment. "I'm afraid so."

"So, you're too smart to make that move."

"I knew you'd agree."

"Wrong. No agreement in this corner. I say, tell him how you feel and let the chips fall. All men are phobic when it comes to commitment. If you don't step out, Danni, you'll never know if you were the one who could make him *want* to settle down."

"This is easy for you. You've found the right guy."

"Wrong again, Sis. Steve quit calling two weeks ago. No argument, nothing. He suddenly just quit being there."

Danni's jaw figuratively hit the floor. "You're kidding."

"Nope. But, at least I had a wonderful time while it lasted."

Danni knew Tess was upset, but decided against talking anymore about it. She'd give her sister time to heal, when the time was right, Tess would spill all.

It did make her think, though.

Should she let Mike into her heart? If she did, would he want to stay?

"Let's get the business out of the way. Is Sallie going to let Joe have Joey over on the sixth?"

"She said she'd need to be able to relax. How about a cruise?"

"No problem. Joe said whatever it took was fine with him."

Danni pulled her briefcase from her desk and sat next to Michael on the couch. "I found what we kept overlooking."

Michael looked so good sitting on her couch. Like he belonged there. She'd actually invited him into her den, in the downstairs portion of her home. "Really? I'm impressed. What is it?"

"There's no social security number for Joey on any of our documents. When I question Sallie, she keeps putting me off when I ask for records of any kind, birth, shot, school, anything."

She handed copies of all the pages that should have had the information on it from all the different papers that each of them had filed.

Why couldn't you be a hundred and twenty pounds overweight with a face only a mother could love? No, you have to be tall and muscular and have blue eyes and jet-black hair and . . . all that makes a woman want to say yes to you. She looked him over while Michael looked over the forms.

After a thorough examination, he met her gaze. "You're right. What could that mean? Have they never claimed the child on their taxes?"

"Sallie brought me the last three years' tax documents. No, they haven't."

"Doesn't that strike you as odd?" When he looked at her with those deep blue eyes, she wanted to crawl over the papers and just touch his face. Not even a kiss. Just a touch. That's all she needed.

She cleared her throat, hoping her thoughts would follow. "Under most circumstances I wouldn't bring this up to my opposition. But, I thought we both needed to know this."

"Well, you're right, we need to examine the situation."

She put all the documents back into her briefcase, closed it, and sat it on the floor. "So, is that it?"

He became intense, suddenly, as if there were something more than the case at stake. "Danni, I want to get this thing over with as soon as possible. So, I looked over everything, thought of every angle and this is what I came up with."

"I'm still listening."

"Let's meet with both parties, and the child. We'll both interview each one, including Joey. After that, we'll decide whether we need to go to court, or we can settle beforehand."

She tried to sound casual. "That sounds fair. This week is good for me, I'm only in court on Wednesday."

"I'll get the meeting together, then, with that in mind."

She got to her feet. "I appreciate you coming by."

He picked up his briefcase and got ready

to leave. He towered over her when he stood beside her. "I'll call you as soon as I get a time. Oh, and Danni, when this is over, I get a date."

"We'll see."

He grinned, wryly. "How did I know you were going to say that?"

"You obviously have a sixth sense for these things."

"You're right, you know. I can see us sitting at The Ramsey eating steaks and having a great time."

"Oops, you just told the past, not the future."

He cocked his head as if he knew a secret. "Are you saying you had a great time?"

She stepped back to let him pass her. "I'm saying we've already been to The Ramsey. Good-bye, Mike. Call me when you get the meeting together."

He walked to the stairs, but turned back around and looked at her. "I certainly hope you don't think this dismissal of me hurts my feelings or deters my pursuit of your company?"

"I wouldn't dream of hurting your feelings. As for the latter, yes."

"We'll see."

Chapter Nine

Sallie Fairmont didn't even pretend the cruise was just a deception to get her out of town while her husband had Joey. She accepted it and went without further question.

Danni, however, simmered with anger. The couple had no scruples whatsoever. Neither one of them. Tired and disheartened, she looked over her messages.

One of them was from her supervisor. He gave her the retainer on the largest account she'd had yet. *This day may turn out to be a good one, after all.* As she filtered through her mail, Mr. Greene entered her small office.

"You're doing us a good job, Danielle. We're all very proud of you."

"Please, sit down, Mr. Greene. Thank you for your support. I'm honored you'd trust me with the DeWitt retainer."

"John DeWitt asked for you after he saw you on the news. With Thomas Reed retiring he wanted new blood on it." He held a file in his hands. "The Fairmont case going as planned?"

"I think we have a good chance of winning it, sir."

"I like to hear that. Of course, anything can happen," he reminded her.

"I know. I just have a good feeling about it."

"Danielle, Mr. Smelcer and I have been talking. We've decided to give you the Winters case."

"Excuse me?" She couldn't have heard him right. This case belonged to Hugh. Danni knew that. "But, Hugh Cramer is next in line, isn't he?"

"Cramer is working on a huge work comp case for AdCo, that's going to be taking all his time. We talked about it, we thought we'd let you run with this."

She now had to follow up her dazzling performance on the Dogwood Manor case. To be honest, it frightened her.

Mr. Greene informed her of the assignment. "Cal Winters is going toe-to-toe with Carroll University in Memphis."

"I know the story. He played football, led the team to the Championship that year, and now that his knee is blown, he wants his education. Why did he come to the other end of the state, for counsel?"

Mr. Greene smiled. "Because his father and I are best friends. Have been since college."

"The precedent on this type of thing is hazy. Some have been awarded this, others haven't."

"You'll be lead counsel, but John Thompson, who knows the Memphis system well, will work with you. He's overnighting all the documents today. It's your baby," Mr. Greene told her, "And, you need to rock it."

Danni smiled. "Thank you for your confidence."

"One reason I told you today is you're

going to need to be in Memphis the day after tomorrow for a press conference."

He left her on that note.

Press conference. What was she getting into?

Hugh walked through the door. "So, are you headed to Memphis?"

"It looks like I am. Are you okay with this?"

He shrugged. "I didn't want to tell you this, but I had first choice."

He didn't tell her anything she didn't already know. "You didn't take it . . . because?"

Hugh's countenance changed. This wasn't the easygoing guy she was used to confiding in. In fact, she became wary as he spoke. "The comp case is a sure thing. You're walking a thin line."

She studied him a long moment. "I suppose so." He didn't answer her, just sat down and looked around the room as if he wanted to tell her something and didn't know how.

A quick and disturbing thought entered Danni's mind. "Do you think if I lose I'm fired?"

He waved his hands in a dismissive gesture. "I'm not the final word on that by any stretch of the imagination. But, even though this is an important case, it's no more important than others on the books right now. You win some, you lose some. That's just life and luck in the courtroom. You draw a judge who hates you. You draw a judge who doesn't like the case. It's not a situation that would make me uncomfortable."

Disconcerted, Danni crossed her arms and looked pointedly at him. "Hugh, if this is how you really feel, then why am I headed to Memphis this week?"

He got up from his seat and closed the door. "I'm leaving, Danni. As soon as the AdCo thing is closed, I'm going into criminal law at Stevens and Burns."

"But, you're in line for the next partnership."

"I know. But, it's what I've always wanted."

She nodded toward the door. "I assume it's a secret."

"Yeah. I trust you, though."

She sidled up beside him and placed her hand on his arm. "I'll miss you."

"Me, too."

As if all had been said that needed to be, Hugh left. Danni, though uneasy about the whole situation, resolved to be the best she could. It was all anyone could do.

Her phone buzzed. "Danni, Michael Sommers on line three."

"Danielle Price."

She could hear the grin in Michael's tone. "I'm looking over some of the Fairmonts' forms and need to know."

"Know? Know what?" She couldn't help but smile herself.

"Your middle name. You sign everything Danielle B. Price."

"None of your business."

"That starts with an N. Listen, I had this idea—good grief! Danni, your picture is on the local news."

She got her remote from the desk drawer and flipped on the small television she kept in her office. "What channel?"

"Seven. What have you done now?"

The newscaster that Mr. Fairmont dated gave the story. "Fort White attorney Danielle Price who is still resting on her laurels from the Dogwood Manor case will be representing Cal Winters in his case against Carroll University. Miss Price will be in

Memphis on Friday to talk with the press per our sources on the case."

Michael sounded hurt. "I'm surprised you didn't tell me."

"I found out about it approximately ten minutes ago. That gal is good. She must have known before I did."

"It's a good case, Danni. Win it, and you've paid your dues. And, you're just starting year number two. You should be ecstatic."

"I'm afraid to talk to you. I'm scared the line is bugged after knowing she knew before I did."

"Tomorrow, after we get the Fairmonts squared away, we'll talk and you can tell me all about it."

"Tomorrow?"

"Be in my office at five o'clock, and we'll get this thing done. I'm looking forward to a steak and some peace of mind."

Danni couldn't help but huff. "I'm not sure we'll ever get the latter."

"Hello, Miss Price. Mr. Sommers called to say he would be a little late. He's in Clifton on a deposition, but he's on his way." Michael's secretary showed Danni into the conference room. She laid her briefcase on the table and looked out the window that offered a view of the courthouse. The peaceful scene didn't calm her nerves.

She had to put her feelings for Michael aside and win this case. Period.

Joe Fairmont arrived first. He sat in the chair at the head of the conference table at Cole, Sommers, and Sommers. He was loud, obnoxious, and thought all things should always go his way—Danni could see this would be a fight to the finish. She wondered why Cole, Sommers, and Sommers would keep him as a client even with his money. How much more of an overbearing idiot could he be?

Danni chose a seat several chairs away from Joe and sat down, trying to ignore his rude comments.

Joe rambled on regarding the case. "So, I told her if she wanted out, she could go with what she came in with, Miss Price. And, that's what Mr. Sommers and I are here to do, today. Make sure you and that tramp leave with nothing."

Danni became incensed. "Why did you marry Mrs. Fairmont?"

"Pardon?"

"Well, you must have seen something in her when you married her, Mr. Fairmont. Now, you sit here and try to make me think you have no fault in this situation. I think we both know better, though, don't you?"

Before the sputtering Mr. Fairmont could finish a sentence, Michael walked through the door. He looked to Joe. "Sorry, I'm late. Traffic was horrible with the bridge out, and I was in Clifton County."

Danni leaned forward on the table. "Don't worry, Mr. Sommers, your client and I had an interesting conversation about why we marry who we do."

Red-faced, Joe addressed Mike. "I want you to do whatever you have to do to get my boy for me, do you hear me?"

Danni answered him, "Mr. Fairmont, unless your attorney is deaf, he heard you, in fact, I'd say the attorneys down the hall heard you as well."

"You think you're ready to take on Joseph Fairmont, Miss Price? You win one big case and you feel as if you rule the world, well let me tell you, you haughty little—"

Michael interrupted him. "That's enough."

He looked at Danni with an arched brow as if to warn her to stop, as well.

Joe's nostrils flared and reminded her of a horse she'd ridden at the state fair as a child.

Unscathed, she could only try to hide the wry grin that pulled at the corners of her mouth as she sank back into the overstuffed leather chair.

Both she and Michael waited quietly for Mrs. Fairmont to show. Joe picked up a magazine and read it. The boardroom in Mike's office was the size of a small house. She envied his position. But, as her mind drifted to the Winters case, she wondered if she'd have something like this in the future.

After about ten minutes, she could hear high-heeled shoes tapping on the hardwood floors in the hall, approaching the room where they waited. Another lighter tapping that she couldn't identify had to be the shoes of the little boy.

But, she wasn't exactly right about that part.

Sallie had the leash of a small potbellied pig. It wore a Tennessee University bright blue sweater, and a matching cap with little holes poked through it to allow his ears to perk up. His jeans let his curly tail through, too.

Danni leaned toward Sallie as the pig climbed into the chair between them. "Where's Joey?"

"This is my Joey. Isn't mommy's boy beautiful?" Sallie gave the pig a big kiss on his snout.

Joey snorted.

So did Mr. Fairmont. "Do you see how she acts? As if she cares! You only want him because he makes money for the company."

Sallie retaliated, "That's the only reason *you* want him. I want him because he's my baby." She gave the pig a bite of an apple she took from a small diaper bag she carried with her.

The pig took the bite and looked around the room as if he knew exactly what was happening around him.

Danni thought aloud, "We need to reset this thing in property."

Mike stared at Joey, baffled.

Mr. Fairmont began the argument. "You

aren't getting Joey, Sallie. But, I'll pay you what he's worth."

"As a pig, maybe. But, not as *my baby*." She stroked Joey to make her point.

"*Your* baby, my grandmother's girdle. You didn't even notice him until he started making money for the company."

Danni took a deep breath. "What do the two of you want?"

"What's best for Joey, of course," Sallie stated.

"I want the pig for my company. He's a good pet, but she only wants him to get back at me."

Sallie retorted, "He only wants him for the money."

Michael hadn't said a word and when Danni looked over to him, she noticed he'd paled slightly. "I think that Joe and I will step down to my office for a moment, if you'll excuse us."

When the men left, Danni resisted the impulse to choke Sallie. Instead, her tone harsh, she told her, "Don't give me any crap, Sallie. I need the truth. Do you want the pig, or do you want money?"

Sallie faltered.

Danni lowered her voice in quiet emphasis. "Just be straight with me, I'll get you what you want, but I need to know what it *really* is."

Sallie's complete countenance changed, even her sweet voice turned coarse. "Show me the money."

"How much will it take?"

Sallie gave her a number.

"Fine, follow my lead."

After Michael led Joe to his office, he closed the door and sat down behind his desk. "*That's* Joey?" he finally asked.

Joe's answer was matter-of-fact. "He's my boy. He's the Fairmont Farms logo. I like him and want him with me."

Michael let his anger into his tone of voice with no remorse. "Joe, you have Cole, Sommers, and Sommers as well as Smelcer and Greene fighting this out in a custody battle."

Annoyance flashed in the man's eyes and voice. "I want my pig!"

"That's all well and good. But, you've got the two top law firms in the city in family court with a piece of property, not a child. You may be attached to the little fellow, but legally, we're not even in the right ball park."

"I don't care what game you have to play, Mike. Get me my pig!"

Michael looked at his client with doubt. "You want him for your company. If I get him, how will he live?"

Joe's countenance softened. "I'll keep him well, Mike. I won't let anything happen to him."

"And, when he's no longer the company mascot, then what?"

"You've seen my farm. He'll always have anything he could want."

Disgusted, Michael threw the pencil he held in his hand on the desk. "Fine! I'll get you your pig, but I'm going to tell you now, you'll pay dearly for him."

Joe looked at him with a grin. "I don't think so, Mike. I think you can get him for me for nothing."

"I don't work miracles."

Joe's smile widened. "Just tell them we'll settle next week."

I don't even want to know what this guy is thinking. Danni will be all over this.

The men returned to the scene of the crime.

Before the door closed, Danni stood. "Mr. Fairmont, as you know, you are to take Joey with you from this meeting for visitation. Mrs. Fairmont has authorized me to negotiate from here. If you'll allow us, I believe Mr. Sommers and I can suggest a reasonable settlement within a few days."

Joe looked at his attorney with a sly grin.

Michael nodded.

The Fairmonts, after much ado about whatever they could think of to fight about, left their attorneys to the business of breaking up their marriage.

Michael sat down across from Danni. "He still wants full custody."

"So does she."

They both sat quiet for a moment.

Michael broke the silence. "All joking aside, let me think this out. Joe doesn't want to pay anything. But, since that's just not realistic, what do you think it would cost to buy Joey's custody from Sallie?"

Danni smirked. "What makes you think she's willing to give him up?"

He sat back and studied her. "My guess is you took the time while we were in my office and asked her for a figure. Tell me what it is and I'll talk to Joe about it."

Danni knew exactly what she would say, but she waited a long moment to give Michael the impression of insecurity. When someone went up against a stronger opponent, she wanted to be underestimated.

The figure she gave him was Sallie's number plus fifty thousand.

"No way. I'll give you this." He wrote a number on a piece of paper. It equaled Sallie's figure plus twenty thousand.

"You really think he'll give her the money?"

Mike shrugged. "He'll have to. In some ways, this thing is bigger than custody."

She smiled. "Okay, then. Throw in a mud allowance and you have a deal, Mr. Sommers."

He met her gaze with a boyish grin, which turned into a chuckle.

Danni tried to suppress a giggle that turned into a peal of laughter. She wiped tears from her eyes, as her side ached. "He's a pig, Mike. A little, cute, Tennessee University fan pig."

Mike walked with what appeared to be great effort through his own laughter, to where she sat. Still trying to control himself, he told her, "Danni, I'm not sure if we're in the midst of a great case over a popular company mascot or a piggy custody battle that could ruin us."

"Then, shouldn't we quit laughing like hyenas?"

As the laughter died Michael spoke, "This is over, Danni. The Fairmont case is over." With those words he took Danni in his arms and kissed her.

She liked the feel of his firm, warm lips on hers.

Danni's voice, husky from the emotion the kiss evoked told him, "It's a good thing we were able to come to an agreeable resolution."

"I know."

Snugly wrapped in his arms, a security seeped through her veins. As if she belonged there, in his arms.

His voice sent a ripple of contentment through her. "I have to go to Nashville this weekend."

She sighed. "I'll be in Memphis."

"Monday night okay with you, then?"

"I'll cook." Danni couldn't believe she was being so amenable.

He smiled. "I'll just bet you will."

"Chicken breast filets. I keep them in my

freezer." Her humor eased the tension in the room.

"So I've been told."

Another quick kiss and Michael excused himself. "I've got a hundred things to get done before I leave."

Danni put everything back in her briefcase. "I know. So do I." She hesitated. "Michael?"

"Yeah, Hon?"

She had to know. "Is this real?"

The warmth of his smile echoed in his voice. "Oh, yes. Very real."

Danni wished she had a Jaguar for every time she walked through the halls of the county courthouse. The secretary who usually did all the filings was out with a case of summer cold and Danni volunteered to walk across the street and do some paperwork.

She wanted to get out and walk. Think. Now that the Fairmont case was all but settled, Danni could see Mike. They could be together and it wouldn't be a conflict of interest.

The courier bag should be in her box when she returned to work and she'd start on her next big case. With these thoughts her life, both professionally and personally, took flight.

Someone calling her name interrupted her reflections.

"Danielle?"

When she turned around Sharon Garrett stood there, looking beautiful in a green suit with gold trim. "I thought that was you."

Stunned, Danni had no idea what to say to a woman whose boyfriend she'd just been kissing last evening. "Hello, Sharon. How are you?"

Her green eyes glittered, mischievously. "I just won the case I came here for, so I'm feeling *good*. You want to catch some lunch? I hate eating alone."

Danni swallowed hard. This couldn't be any worse.

"Have you eaten?"

"No." *Why didn't I just say yes?*

"Great, let's go, then."

At the Soup Kitchen, they got their meals, Sharon picking up the tab, explaining that since she'd shanghaied Danni into eating with her, that was the least she could do.

"So," Sharon said between bites, "what's the deal with you and the guy at the opera?"

"Hugh? We're friends. I'm not interested in him at all."

Sharon cast Danni a knowing look. "Does he feel the same way?"

Danni nodded. "Exactly the same way. What about Mike Sommers?"

Sharon put her spoon down. "Oh, I love him. How couldn't someone love him?"

How, indeed? Danni thought Sharon's words would gag her.

Sharon continued, "He's the sweetest guy on earth." Danni noticed the delicate ring on her lunch mate's finger, an engagement ring.

"So, you've known him a long time?"

"Seems like forever. We've been close since college. He's always there when I need him. Like I said, he's just a really nice guy."

Yeah, a nice guy who's engaged to you and dating me. A great guy, all right.

Her cell phone ringing saved Danni. "Hello?"

"Danni, it's Mike. How are you?"

She became edgier each minute, as her dismay grew. "Fine, Mike. And, you?"

"Your voice sounds funny, are you all right?"

"I'm great. Just kind of busy, I'll catch you later, okay?"

"Okay, but call me later, will you? I don't want to leave without seeing you."

"That's not going to be possible. But, I'll see you Monday, as we planned."

She could hear the confusion and hurt even on the bad connection. "Okay, well, I'll see you then. Take care."

She flipped the phone shut.

Sharon didn't catch onto anything. "You and Mike are opposing right now, aren't you?"

"Yes. That was a date—I mean appointment—"

"Don't let him fool you, Danni, he's a killer in the courtroom."

She only half listened as she struggled with her conscience. "Yes, I've heard."

Sharon chuckled. "Of course, you beat his dad. That was news."

"It was a good case. No one else in town would touch it. I admit it, winning felt good."

"Well, of course it did. You did a great job. Danni, aren't you hungry? You haven't touched your soup and it's wonderful."

Danni stood. "I had a big breakfast and really need to get back to work. It was good seeing you again, Sharon."

Sharon returned her smile. "Same here. Hope to see you again. In fact, you're invited to the wedding." Sharon flashed her ring.

"I'll look forward to the invitation."

Danni wandered back to the courthouse to do what she'd went there for when she saw Sharon. After all documents were filed, she walked back to the office in a daze. Michael had made it clear he wanted to see her romantically and all the while he planned to marry Sharon. She should have been furious. She should have called him and told him exactly where he could stick his intentions.

However, anger didn't hit her as hard as the hurt did. She'd wanted to think Tess had been right and he cared about her. Or, at least, she had a chance of him caring.

When she got to the office, she sat down, and looked around it. Piled sky high was work that needed her immediate attention.

She tried to concentrate, to no avail.

Instead, she went home a little early and sat in her kitchen, rubbing the dog's head and hoping for a better feeling.

The phone rang, and upon checking the caller ID, she knew it was Tess. Talking to her sister was the last thing she wanted right now. She let the machine pick it up.

After a bath and some dinner, she went into the downstairs den and turned on the television. Something she hadn't done in months. Concentration eluded her.

When the phone rang, she didn't go to the kitchen to check the ID, but answered it.

"Hello."

She knew who it was before she heard his warm, rich voice. "Hello, Danni. It's Michael."

In spite of her reserve, a tinge of anxiety came into her tone. "What's going on?"

He sighed in exasperation. "Joe is not happy with the settlement."

"I don't care if he's happy, only if he took it."

"Not while he still draws a breath."

Sternly, she ground out her words. "What does he want, Michael, just tell me."

The words were playful, but his meaning was not. "He wants to walk away, pig neatly in the poke, and never see or hear from Sallie for as long as they both shall live."

She rolled her eyes. "You and I both know Sallie won't buy that. We need to do something or we'll be working this case from a nursing home."

"You're right. I've thought about this all afternoon, and nothing I've recommended made it past the 'while he was alive' part of the conversation."

She didn't try to hide the contempt. "Did you tell him I could arrange that?"

"Your father is a cop, remember? Think of the publicity."

She heard a touch of humor in her own voice. "Think of all the bad guys he knows. Anyway, exactly what have you discussed? Is there anything I can work with on my end?"

"No. He won't budge. This is why I hate divorce cases. Property settlements take forever."

She pursed her lips. "The paperwork is on my secretary's desk to get this moved *from* custody *to* property."

"That's certainly the only way to start. At least, if the press should get a hold of this, we don't look like the idiots we've made ourselves out to be."

"Exactly. Just remember, look for the social security number on all custody suits. This will be a lesson to both of us."

Impatience threaded his tone. "But, after that, we're still back to the big bad wolves fighting for one little pig."

She spoke the next words with authority and articulation. "The truth is, Michael, we may just have to go into court and fight it out."

Suddenly, he sounded tired. "I hate for it to come to that."

"I'm past caring."

Michael found the comment out of character. "Danni? Are you okay? You sound a little . . . I don't know, strange."

She tried to pass off the comment. "I am strange. I thought you knew that."

An awkward moment passed. When he spoke again, she heard a tenderness that hadn't been there a moment ago. "I know this settlement business hasn't done either of us any good. But, we'll get this moved from child custody, to take that heat off, and we'll be fine. You know that, don't you? That we'll be okay?"

She sounded unconvinced. "Sure."

"Are you sick?"

"Not really, but to make sure, you could come over and press a cold piece of chicken against my eye."

Good. She made a joke, so she must be all right. "Ah, yes. You love to bring that up, don't you?"

She didn't answer him.

"Danni? Are you still there?"

"Yeah." She sounded strained. "But, I *do* have a headache, Michael."

"Then, I should let you go."

"I think I'll go to bed early. See you soon."

"You too." Michael hung up the phone with a feeling of dread in his stomach. Something was wrong. Extremely wrong. Something had happened between them and he didn't even know the reason. It hung in the air like a bad odor. He went over the last conversation they'd had before tonight. All was well when he'd talked with her before.

He'd jump off each bridge as he came to it. Since they were both leaving for the weekend tomorrow, he'd have to wait to see her. Come Monday, all would be set right.

The feel of her lips still made his warm. He wasn't going to lose her. Not now.

Chapter Ten

Monday morning, her phone buzzed first thing. "Danni, line three is Michael Sommers."

"Can you put that though to my voice mail, Bonnie?"

Bonnie sounded incredulous. "You want *him* on your *voice mail?*"

"Yes. Please." Her own clipped words made her cringe. She didn't want to hurt her secretary's feelings. "I just need to get a handle on things from the weekend, Bonnie."

Bonnie seemed reassured by her answer. "On your voice mail, it is."

Danni admitted one thing. She had no idea what she should do. Should she confront him? Should she just lay low? She mindlessly shuffled papers for about ten minutes, then checked her voice mail.

The automated operator gave its usual spiel, "You have one new message, the message is: "Danielle, it's Michael. I have this feeling something's wrong, but I don't know how to fix it. Please call me today if you get the chance. I'd like to know if we're still on for dinner and get this Fairmont thing finalized so we can get on with our lives. I can't get our kiss out of my mind." He chuckled. "I certainly hope you check your own voice mail. Anyway, call me."

She erased the message and put the phone back on the hook.

All weekend all she thought about was what Sharon told her. He'd gone to Nashville for the weekend, probably for an engagement party.

No, he'd get no call until there was a business reason to do so. She wanted no part of Michael Sommers.

Michael wouldn't step one foot on her doorstep.

Back to work. Her Memphis trip had been an adventure to say the least. All those debating and public speaking classes she'd taken throughout her high school and college years certainly paid off. She was aware the Winters case meant high profile.

And, now she knew what the words "high" profile really meant. When she stepped off the plane and faced the bombardment of questions from the actual melee of radio, TV, and newspapers blinded her with lights, camera flashes, and yelling. Microphones stuck nearly in her mouth and a constant barrage of noise left her a little off-kilter. She retained her composure, however, and upon her return yesterday, had a message waiting on her home phone from Mr. Greene.

He sounded as excited as he ever did. Which wasn't much, but still a good sign that she handled Memphis well.

Danni's secretary stepped inside her door after knocking. "Danni, Vickie Sawyer from Channel Seven is here."

Not again. "The Winters thing?"

"No." Obviously, the newswoman troubled Bonnie. "It's about the Fairmont case."

Danni didn't try to hide her shock. "What?"

"Yeah. Do you want to talk with her? She's got the cameras and microphones set up, Danni. It looks as if it could get ugly."

Hugh buzzed her. "Danni, pick up."

She plucked up the headset so no one else could hear their conversation.

"The reception area looks like something P.T. Barnum would think of, what's the deal?"

"The Fairmont case. I thought we'd get it settled before something like this happened. I don't even know what it's about. But, I don't like it, because Joey Fairmont turned out to be a pig."

Hugh's confusion was apparent, even by phone. "*What?*"

Her sentence sounded choppy to her own ears. "You know, one of those little pet pigs."

"But, you're fighting custody on this, Danni. The press is going to bury you and Sommers."

With more confidence than she really had, she told him, "No, I had Bonnie change it from custody to property on Friday. We're set."

"When did you find time to do that?"

"I left her a message on Thursday evening. In fact, the paper work is here on my desk now." She looked it over.

Cold dread poured over her.

Holding the phone against her chest to muffle her yell, she called her secretary into the office. "Bonnie, did you take the Fairmont file to the courthouse on Friday?"

"No. I had the day off, remember?"

Hugh walked through the door as Bonnie answered her.

"Come in, please, Bonnie." Danni hung up the phone. *Okay, now what?* She addressed her assistant. "First, tell Miss Sawyer to meet me at three o'clock at Cole, Sommers, and Sommers. We'll have a statement for her. Then, Bonnie, please take this to the courthouse and stop for nothing."

Hugh turned pale on her behalf. "Oh, no. If the media finds it out, you and Sommers are ruined."

Sommers.

Pressing Bonnie to run, she lifted the handset to call Michael.

Mike expected to hear from Danni, but

not in this mood. "I'm Danielle Price and Houston we have a problem."

"What's wrong Danni, why haven't you answered—"

She interrupted him. "That's not important. I just had my secretary chase Vickie Sawyer out of the reception area. She was loaded for pig, too. Wanted information on the Fairmonts. What do you know about this?"

Michael sat up in his chair. "Not a thing. We'd better chase down our clients."

"Mine's on a cruise, so call me as soon as you hear from yours. Oh, and Vickie expects a release of information at three o'clock at your office."

Michael groaned. "Why would she expect *that*?"

"Because I told her to meet us there."

"*Because?*"

Danni's voice held no apology. "It was the only thing I could think of to get rid of her."

"Then, I'd better find Joe Fairmont."

"Good idea."

They rang off. Michael had his secretary, Carol, call everyone he could think of to find Fairmont. If Danni hadn't had this moved from custody, they'd both have been ruined.

His father entered the room in a hurry. "What's happening out there? Your secretary looks like she's been hit with a bomb and the receptionist is trying to answer the phone and dust."

"Carol is trying to find Fairmont for me. I'm coming up with a settlement he's going to agree to, and Joey Fairmont is a pig."

"I raised you better than that."

Michael turned from the forms on his desk to face his father. "No, you don't get it, Dad. He *is* a pig. One of those cute, little potbellied pigs. In fact, he's the one they use in the commercials."

His father stared at him. "Mike, that's not custody, it's personal property."

"Tell me about it. When the legal community hears about this, I'm ruined. And, on top of all that guess who's coming here at three o'clock?"

"Don't tell me. Pete Randall?" His father shook his head in dismay.

Michael could have killed Joe when he thought about this whole thing. "Wrong station. No, it's Vickie—oh, what's her name."

"It doesn't matter. You're between a rock and a hard place. You can't give out any information. You can't find your client, and what about Miss Price?"

"Oh, Sallie's in the Bahamas on a cruise. This is Joe's idea to ruin her while she's gone."

His father actually yelled, "Is he crazy?"

"Maybe. But, Joe's dating Vickie and . . . Joe's dating Vickie." Michael slowed down, took a deep breath and spoke, "Son of a gun. Okay, fine." He pushed the button on his phone. "Carol, forget finding Joe Fairmont. Get me Miss Price on the phone."

His father asked, "Are you sure of your information?"

"Oh, yes. Very sure."

His phone buzzed. "Miss Price isn't in her office."

"Tell her secretary to find her at all costs. Then, get me Vickie Sawyer on the line."

Carol's shocked tone met his ears. "Vickie Sawyer? At the television station?"

"One and the same."

His phone buzzed. "Michael, Joe Fairmont on line three for you."

He sat down in his chair, and answered the phone. "This is Michael Sommers."

Joe Fairmont sounded pleased with himself. "Mike, good! You're there. I had a great idea."

He couldn't stop the sarcasm that dripped from his lips. "Yes, I'm here. Let me guess about this great idea of yours. Vickie Sawyer showed up at Greene and Smelcer today to speak with Miss Price. Your doing?"

"Sure was. Sorry, Mike, but I didn't feel like you were getting it done. You just couldn't pull this off on your own."

Disgust filled Michael. "If you didn't want me on this, why didn't you ask my father—"

"After he'd just lost that big case over that house to the Price woman? No way. I knew that I'd have to handle this in the end, and that's what I'm doing."

"You want Miss Price and me to talk to Vickie Sawyer, on live television? That's your big plan that's going to guarantee you get what you want?"

"This pig is my company. When we started using him in commercials, our vegetables flew off the shelves like they had wings. No one is going to wreck that for me. Especially, Sallie."

"You should have left the situation to the professionals. What do you expect me to say at this press conference?"

"I'll be there. We'll talk about the settlement. We'll tell the sad story of how Sallie is taking me for a bundle so I can keep Joey." Joe thought he had it all figured out by his speech.

"Why did you send the press to Sallie's attorney? What on earth did you expect her to say?"

"I just wanted the press to go there and see that Price wasn't willing to talk. It makes a person look bad when all the media gets is a no comment."

Carol knocked, then walked through the opened doorway. "Miss Price is here."

"Have her wait a moment." Then, back to Joe. "You can't do this. We *can't* go on television."

The determined answer he received angered him more. "Yes we can. And, we will."

Joe hung up before Michael could say anything.

Danni burst through the door, pointing at the phone. "Is that your client?"

Michael hung up the phone. "It *was*."

"He is such a low life. I can't believe he'd do this." She paused to catch her breath. "Michael, this is not just bad, it's worse."

"Oh, no. Please don't tell me. You weren't able to get this changed from custody, were you?"

"Bonnie is on her way right now."

"But, any papers that are on file—and Vickie Sawyer would have copies of them, furnished by Joe—would be on custody."

Danni added the rest. "And *we* look like idiots. Can you reach Joe again?"

With a sigh, Michael told her, "I can try."

"I want to talk to him."

Michael called Joe at his office. He answered the phone sounding smug. "Joe Fairmont, here."

"Mr. Fairmont, Michael Sommers, again. Miss Price is with me. She wanted to speak to you." Michael flipped the speakerphone button.

"Miss Price, I'm sure you have something you'd *like* to say, I doubt it would sound professional, however." The man was so full of himself.

"I wanted to have your attorney present when we spoke, Mr. Fairmont, any chance you'd meet us here?"

"None. I'll do all my talking a little later with the cameras on."

Danni laid it on thick. "No, you won't, Mr. Fairmont. You're not going on local T.V. to slander your wife."

"It's only slander if I can't prove it."

"Mr. Fairmont, on the night of the twenty-sixth, I met with your attorney and came up with a reasonable—"

"Reasonable, my granny's house dress! You're just like that trollop, and you're not getting a cent."

Danni leaned on the desk near the phone for what would have been a great show of determination had Joe been there to see it. "Then, let me make this perfectly clear, Mr. Fairmont. I want to make sure you're listening very close."

Sounding unscathed at her words, he answered her, "Oh, I *am* listening Miss Price."

"Good. I know you. I know your habits. Now, if you get in front of the cameras and start throwing stones, I will burn you to a crispy, crackling, crunch. You and your little anchor girl, too."

Joe didn't seem so untouched by her words. "Is that a threat?"

Danni stood straight. "No, sir. A *threat* is something I don't intend to carry out. I have all intentions of keeping this *promise*."

"I'll see you there at three o'clock." Fairmont hung the phone up.

Danni looked at Michael. "I'm sorry, Michael."

Michael could see a chill in her eyes he'd never seen before. "What are you going to do?"

"Do you remember the first night we met? You said something to me. I'll never forget it."

Michael tried to lighten the mood. "Did it start 'Confucius says'?"

"You said that in the courtroom I was just another attorney. I'm sorry." She left before he could say more.

His phone buzzed. "Miss Sawyer on line two for you, Michael."

Just another godforsaken day in paradise.

Danni returned to the offices where Michael's family had practiced law for three generations. She'd done some finagling in the interim of the morning and the afternoon. For one thing, she did have the case moved from custody to property. The papers were filed, but that didn't mean it wouldn't be a thorn in the flesh with the press if the wrong people knew about it.

And, they probably did.

She thought about Vickie Sawyer and Joe Fairmont, all snuggled together in the diner. Danni knew enough about the business to see a set up when it hit her in the face.

But, she resolved that the opposition would not run the show.

Not beyond a little "setting up" of her own, she had another ace up her sleeve. Pete Randall, station owner at Channel Eleven, would also send a news team. Now, Joe and Vickie would have to share the spotlight. She'd have her own circus to ringmaster.

When Danni entered the foyer, there were at least twenty people milling around. "Here she comes!" It was Vickie who poked a microphone in her face and asked, "Is it true Mr. Fairmont will prove your client unfit?"

Danni walked to a lectern set in anticipation of this briefing. Michael and his father were present, as she knew they would be. She didn't allow Miss Vickie to get her in a bad position. She'd spoken with Sallie from the cruise ship. Since her client couldn't be there, it was understood she would handle the situation any way she saw fit.

"Miss Sawyer, if you'll excuse me, I have a statement for the media." She saw Pete Randall in the audience. He didn't send a flunky; he came to see this for himself. For a brief second, Danni wondered why.

"Sallie Rutherford Fairmont is not here today. She is out of town, and has asked me as her counsel to make a statement and field any questions from the press."

Questions started to fly from the six or so reporters that had gathered. The two local papers and all three of the local television stations, plus one or two of the radio stations were present.

She no longer worried this would get ugly—she worried more about words like hideous and heinous. She motioned for quiet, and then read her statement. "Mrs. Fairmont and her husband, Joseph Fairmont, Jr., were married almost five years ago in a small private ceremony at his home at Baker Hill. At that time, they both knew they'd never have children." She looked to Mr. Fairmont. "I won't go into the medical reasons."

Questions began to fly from the audience.

She once again waved them quiet. "They decided to adopt, but as the marriage started to fall apart, Mrs. Fairmont knew that wouldn't be an option. So, they found Joey."

She pulled a picture of Joey from her briefcase. "As you know, he's now the mascot for Fairmont Farms. I realize you were brought here today under false circumstances. The person who summoned you here told you . . . what? That he would give you a scoop? That you would find out whether or not the rumors are true about his wife?"

She couldn't believe the audience was silent for a long moment.

"This is not a custody suit as you have been told. It's a personal property battle that will leave the winner with a cute pot-bellied pig. That's all. Should Mrs. Fairmont, who loves the pig, or Mr. Fairmont, for whom the pig makes money, be awarded possession? That will be up to a judge to decide. Not the public or the press. I have no further comment."

Vickie still yelled out, "Doesn't Mrs. Fairmont frequent Temptation Alley?"

"I don't, so it would be hard for me to answer that question. However, I do like to run to the Dining Car that's downtown. I go there when I work late, ever been there?"

When Vickie turned fifteen shades of red Danni knew the woman had to know where she was leading. Unfortunately, she didn't back off. "But, you don't know if she hangs out in bars or where she meets men—"

"Miss Sawyer, as I said, this is not about a child, it's about a pet. Personal lives of individuals don't come into play in a personal property dispute or in a divorce filed on the grounds of irreconcilable differences. If you continue to ask such questions, I will have to ask Mr. Sommers to answer the same questions targeted towards Mr. Fairmont. Have I made myself clear?"

Pete Randall jumped into the fray. "So, when did you realize that Joey Fairmont didn't belong in custody, Miss Price? According to public record, there is a custody battle going on here."

"Actually, you're behind times, Mr. Randall. I filed papers earlier clearing up any misunderstandings."

Pete Randall wore a smirk that made his handsome face look contemptuous. "But, your opponent who's been practicing law for several more years than you has missed the fact that this was property and not custody."

"That's not what I said—"

Pete interrupted her. "But he did."

Michael stepped up to the microphone. "We both did. Let's just call a mistake what it is. In their zeal and devotion to little Joey, the Fairmonts think of him as a child."

"But, Mr. Sommers, isn't your firm retained by Fairmont Farms? Why didn't you know who the little guy was?"

Michael sighed. "I have business dealings with Mr. Fairmont. I've never seen the commercials nor been to his home."

Michael came under attack.

Randall became relentless. "Why didn't you know this was a pig and not a child?"

Vickie jumped in. "How much does your client think he'll have to pay to get the pig?"

Another reporter asked, "Will Fairmont Farms continue with your firm if Miss Price beats you in court, like she did your father?"

Yet another voice called out, "Will Joe Fairmont be charged with libel for his interview with *The Hometowner*?"

Danni saw Michael look at Joe on that one. *Oh no*. It was all Danni could do to keep from shaking her head.

The press hounded him regarding the situation as if Danni weren't there and had no fault in it.

She could stay and fight for him.

Or, she could do what any good attorney would do and leave him dangling like a mouse on a string in front of his client and the press.

Michael looked embarrassed. "I am unaware of any interview."

Pete Randall seemed well pleased at the comment. "Your client doesn't tell you everything, then, Sommers. He trashes Sallie Fairmont from here to Memphis."

Michael continued, "As for the firm's association with Fairmont Farms, that's been a staple for both families since before either of us were born."

Vickie asked, "What about the settlement?"

Danni could stand it no longer. She wouldn't let Michael take all the heat.

Yes, a good attorney would. But, she wouldn't. "We haven't reached one as of yet. However, we *are* close. Both parties want to see this settled as soon as possible so our clients can get on with their lives. Also, there is no reason I can think of that Mr. Sommers should take full responsibility for the child versus pig error. Neither of us thought to ask any more questions and took all information at face value. As for this entire situation, many—and I'm sure Mr. Sommers and I can agree on this—

many divorcing couples argue over pets. Don't we all get attached to our animals? I have a dog that I love. So, please, can we keep this to the facts?"

Vickie asked, "But, aren't the facts that Mrs. Fairmont has a life she doesn't want made public?"

"Don't we all, Miss Sawyer?" It was Michael who took this question. "I don't think there's one of us who'd want our private lives on the news. Not because of anything wrong, but if for no other reason, it's no one else's business." Danni was shocked when he added, "If anyone can understand that, Miss Sawyer, you should be able to."

"This is enough," Danni told the press. "Any further questions need to be made in writing. I will choose from that what my client will or will not answer."

Michael looked at Danni as he ushered Joe Fairmont into his office.

Danni tried to leave but Vickie Sawyer cornered her on the sidewalk in front of the firm. "You know Sallie Fairmont is a low life."

Danni grinned wryly. "I know what I saw at the Dining Car that night."

Vickie huffed. "You can't tell that to anyone."

"I am not bound by client-attorney privilege, Miss Sawyer. *Mrs.* Fairmont is my client. If you don't want people knowing then I'd suggest two things. First, be more careful about where you eat and fall all over a married man and second, leave me alone. I may look like a professional in this get-up, but I can unsheathe my claws in record time."

She walked away but wheeled around to face her adversary one last time. "Don't forget that for future reference, by the way."

Pete Randall and his cameral man caught up with Danni as she crossed the street, walking beside her, he asked, "Quite a performance, Miss Price. Did you just give Sawyer the real scoop?"

They reached the other side of the street as Danni turned to him. "Mr. Randall, Vickie Sawyer is the last person to whom I would give any information about this case, my client, or anything else, for that matter. We aren't friends, nor do I scoop about a case."

Pete, who probably had ten years of age

on Danni, could be charming when questioning his prey. "But, someone from your firm made sure Miss Sawyer wasn't the only press at this little shindig."

She cocked her head. "I wouldn't know."

As she tried to walk away from him, Pete grabbed her arm and turned her to face him. "Sure you do. It was you, or someone under your direction. I've seen you in action, Miss Price. You're not a stupid woman, and you're a hell of an attorney."

"I will not be pawed by you, thank you very much." Pete let go as she continued, "I will say this only once. Mr. Sommers—"

Once again he didn't let her finish her sentence. "Which one? The one you crucified a few weeks ago in court, or the one that you just made look like an idiot to the entire city?"

Her head began to throb. "I'll say what I said a few weeks ago to your newsman. Both of them have earned the utmost respect in this town because they deserve it. They are both fine people and jurists. Now, if you will excuse me, I have work to do."

Pete yelled after her, "Good work, Miss Price. You just made my day."

Why did making his day make her feel like a heel?

"What did you do?" Michael asked Joe.

Joe sat back in his chair, obviously feeling very good about himself. "I had a talk with Sherman Phillips over at the paper."

Michael couldn't have been any more disgusted. "*The Hometowner*? Also known as the Fort White Tattle Tale? Joe, tell me you didn't do this."

Joe leaned forward on the Michael's desk. "You still haven't got me what I want. I want my pig, no money down, no payments in the future."

The intercom buzzed. "Michael, I'm bringing in a copy of the article you wanted."

His secretary quietly came in and laid the paper, headline up, on Michael's desk.

"THIS LITTLE PIGGY WENT TO COURT." The story was worse than the title. Michael was appalled as he read how Sallie loved the pig, but Joe wanted him for the company. Everything Joe said sounded like a bad case of sour grapes. Even the picture in the paper, of Sallie with the pig, left people to think she loved the animal.

"This is a backfire. All it looks like is you want the pig for business and Sallie loves him. I don't know if I can undo your damage."

"Damage?" Fairmont grabbed the paper and read the article. "That bum. He turned it all around. I told him exactly what to print. This looks as if he's on her side."

Michael's father, who had stood quietly near the window spoke. "He weighed his stories. Which would sell more papers? The big time businessman hurt by his wife who's trying to get alimony? Or, the hurt damsel in distress who loves a pet because she can't have her own child and the big money man trying to tear it from her arms? Now, which one do *you* think will sell more papers?"

Michael had no doubt his client was not happy when Joe answered. "Humph, I won't give *him* any advertising."

Jason continued. "He'd never have printed that if you'd advertised with him in the first place. Am I right?"

Sitting at his desk, Michael put his hands to his head and told Joe, "Settle. The last price was reasonable for what you're worth and the pig's value to the company."

Joe was quiet a long moment. "Is that your final recommendation?"

Michael looked hard at his client. "Yes, it is."

Joe stood and looked down on Michael. "Then, I'll find myself another attorney. And, not just for this, either. For everything. I should have gotten Sallie's attorney."

Mike got out of his chair to match Joe's height. "Just for your information, Danielle Price can't represent you. It's a conflict of interest."

He leaned toward Michael, poking a finger in his chest across the desk. "No, but she can talk *you* into anything. I just hope that she's worth our retainer."

Michael balked. "Talk me into anything?"

Standing straight back, he told Michael, "You two are in this together, admit it. That's the only explanation for all this."

"You have really gone the way of the wombat. With everything you've done today, you want to blame *me*? You've probably destroyed my career. You've spoiled your *own* chances with the courts." Michael ran his hand through his hair. "I'm telling you as someone who's in this with you to my neck, take the settlement and back off before you ruin yourself."

Michael paused, "Or should I say, before your reputation is damaged further?" He didn't hesitate to glare at Joe firmly. "*You* did this. Only you, and your friend the anchorwoman. You thought you'd take advantage of Sallie being out of town. *You didn't.* You've made things much worse than they ever were. Any judge is going to give her whatever she wants, now. And, it's no one's fault but your own. You deserve whatever the judge does to you."

Joe stormed from the room, slamming the door behind him.

Jason eyed Michael. "He's forgotten something."

"Tell me it's something that means I'm not responsible for our losing the Fairmont retainer."

Jason sat down across from his son. "His father is still alive and won't let him change the retainer. I've already spoken to him."

Relief washed over him. "Thank God."

Jason acted a little nonchalant when he asked, "How do you think Pete Randall caught wind of all this?"

Now Michael concentrated on what he knew the real problem to be. "You and I both know. She wasn't going to be killed in broad daylight on a one-way street."

Jason smiled. "You can't be angry. She did her job. Now, you have to do yours."

His father left him to his thoughts. Michael stood and walked to the window. For a long time he watched the traffic go by two stories down.

Danni had done her job. She even tried to help him at one point in the press conference. Which was all just fine. But, when he was through, Danielle B. Price would be sorry she'd ever met him.

Chapter Eleven

Danni was sorry she ever met Michael Sommers. She hated his position on the other side of the courtroom and for marrying Sharon Garrett.

But, other than those things, she loved him.

Even a hot bath didn't help her with the way she ached. There were so many paths on this trail. And, every one of them led to her destruction.

Her love for him, a man engaged to another woman, a man who was on the opposite side of her court cases.

No way he'd sit back and let her get

away with what she did today. It didn't take a rocket scientist to know she'd tipped off Pete Randall. Or, that she'd answered a few questions for Sherman at that rag of a paper.

Nope. She'd won the battle but the war still raged. When the phone rang, she almost didn't answer but thought, what the heck? She'll have to come out eventually. "Hello."

"Danielle B. Price?"

Michael.

"What is it Michael?"

"I'm calling to tell you I no longer represent Joseph Fairmont in his divorce proceedings."

She sat up in the tub, water sloshing everywhere. "I'm . . . sorry."

"You did the wrong thing, Danielle. Greene will hit the roof when he sees how you took responsibility at the press conference."

She held a hand to her forehead. "Pete Randall tried to make you the butt of the joke. You're not responsible for what happened. At least, not solely."

"Any good attorney would have let me flounder out there, Danni."

"I won't apologize for helping you."

"Greene will cut you in half, you must have known that."

She didn't get the gist of this conversation. "Mike, what's this about? I helped you and now you're mad?"

"Not about the help. I want to know why the rest of the local press was there."

She hesitated. "How should I know?"

"Because you called them and told them to be there, didn't you?

She didn't answer.

Now, his voice held a tinge of anger. "I have to ask how you were able to get to Pete Randall. Oh, let me guess. You mentioned the name Sommers and he jumped to do your bidding."

"I did what I had to do, Michael, you know that. In my defense, I didn't know you and he had a past. Or, that you'd take the heat on the piggy thing. I just assumed we'd both be hit hard on that one."

"Did you see the Tattle Tale?"

"This little piggy and all that? Yes. I know about it."

He remained quiet a moment. "You knew because the source close to Sallie Fairmont mentioned is you."

As much as her heart broke, she wouldn't deny it.

Her silence became her answer.

She heard his sigh over the phone. "Joe thinks we have something going on."

"Then, he's wrong. The only relationship we have is a piggy lawsuit. That's it. We'll cut the settlement by twenty thousand. Talk to Joe."

"Fine. I'll see if he'll still take my calls. Any further communication between *us*, Danni, will be by courier."

"It's for the best."

Michael hung up.

With a heavy heart, Danni got out of the tub, drained it and put on her robe. She couldn't stop the tears, and there was no reason to try.

Danni couldn't have Michael Sommers. She could have her career, the dog, and maybe Tess or her brother Alex would give her nieces and nephews to spoil.

What was wrong with her? Was she crazy? Did it ever really occur to her that she could change the man into someone else? Someone who didn't have a woman in every port? Or, in his case every office of the courthouse?

He'd dated every court clerk, every secretary, and every other attorney in town, with only male exceptions. Why in the world did she think she'd be different?

Because that was his magic, his charm. He made every woman feel special and now, she felt like a special idiot.

She'd come home right after the circus and took the bath to try and relax. But, to no avail.

The television beckoned her to the news. Pete Randall had a field day with Mike.

She sat down and realized that as responsible as she was for this, the least she could do was watch it.

"And, now, the award-winning Eleven Newscast. With Stan Harvey, Lori Hale, Tom Winger on Sports, and Jerry Layman with weather. Here's Lori Hale."

The pretty blonde took over the news. "Today's top story is straight from *The Hometowner.* This morning an article called, "This Little Piggy Went to Court," startled local readers from believing that all was well with a family tradition. With more on the story, our own station manager, Pete Randall."

"Oh, my gosh." Danni spoke the words

aloud. "He'll—he'll . . . ruin Michael. What have I done?"

"As many of you watching tonight know the divorce and,"—he used his fingers to show quote marks—" 'custody battle' between Joseph Fairmont, Jr. and his wife Sallie Rutherford Fairmont has heated up today. An article in *The Hometowner* tells of how Sallie married a wealthy man who doesn't care for their pet pig, Joey. But, since he's become the 'spokes-pig' for his company Fairmont Farms, he's doing all he can to make sure that Mrs. Fairmont never sees the pig again.

"The attorneys who represent both parties held a press conference today. Michael Sommers of Cole, Sommers, and Sommers admitted to not only having no idea the child was a pig, but to never even seeing the commercial."

At this point the press conference played, edited to make Michael look like a complete idiot.

"As we understand it," Mr. Randall went on as the press conference continued silently behind him, "the business between Fairmont Farms and the Sommers law firm has spanned three generations.

"However, possibly the most interesting conversation was one with Danielle Price of Smelcer and Greene, who represents Mrs. Fairmont."

Danni stood from her place on the couch, hand over her mouth.

"I asked her how she felt about the Sommers firm losing the Fairmont Farms retainer and Joe Fairmont losing his prize pig. Her answer?"

He played the part of the tape where she said, ". . . they deserve it."

"No. Oh, no. This can't happen. He butchered the tape. He took the part about respect and made it something awful. Michael will never speak to me again." In fact, the whole family, including a judge she would have to argue in front of, would now hate her. "Nothing could be worse than this."

On that ominous note, her doorbell rang.

When she answered it, Hugh pushed his way in. "You certainly know how to stir a hornet's nest."

"Did you say stir? Inappropriate analogy, Hugh. I plucked it from the tree and used it for a volleyball. The entire town is talking about this and I didn't even say what they claim I said."

Hugh was still obviously having a problem understanding from the confused look on his face.

"How is Mr. Greene taking this?" she asked him.

"He loves the way you've handled it. He doesn't know what I do, though."

Oh, no, what else could there be? "What's that?"

"You tried to save Sommers' butt, didn't you?"

"How did—"

Hugh smiled. "I know that? Oh, I have my sources. I thought you'd go for the gold, but you could have actually done him more harm, if you'd wanted to."

He handed her a copy of the tape from the news station, a copy of the paper, and a copy of the other station's coverage.

After watching that tape, she realized Michael's reputation really was damaged. Vickie interviewed Joe Fairmont, and though the bias was there, it made everything look like Michael's fault, from the newspaper article to the press conference. Joe took no responsibility and presented himself as a man wounded by bad representation.

Lilly, her beloved mutt, strolled into the front room. She sniffed Hugh's feet and he leaned down to pet her head. "Now, what, oh Mistress of Mayhem?"

"I just continue to work. That's all I know to do, unless you have any bright ideas?"

"You've got to be joking. I wouldn't dare give you an idea right now. God only knows what you would do with it."

She sat down. "He's engaged, Hugh."

"Who?"

"Mike. He and Sharon Garrett are engaged."

"No kidding. How do you feel about that?"

She looked up at him.

"Oh. Not good, I see."

"Would you be really hurt if I just wanted to be alone this evening?"

"No. I'll go, if you'll promise to call me if you need me."

She crossed her heart. "Promise made."

Chapter Twelve

The morning sun shone brightly through the glass of Jason Sommers' office.

"You're here early." His father's words cut through his thoughts. The evening before Michael wrote a list of things he would do to make things right with Danni and the Fairmonts. One of those things was to find out his Dad's objections to Danni.

He sat in his father's wing-backed leather chair. "I didn't go home."

"Mike, things happen that we can't do anything about. Joe Senior called me last night. He's upset right now, but not with us. With his son. He's not pulling the re-

161

tainer, and he's not going to give Joe a penny to move the divorce to another lawyer. You're okay."

Michael nodded. "I'm glad to hear that, Dad."

"If this is the happy face, I give up." His dad chided him as if he were a child.

That was the problem, however. "You shouldn't have had to intervene."

"We're still the best firm in town. Don't forget that."

Michael sighed.

"You have other things on your mind, son?"

"Why don't you want me to become involved with Danielle Price?"

Jason laid the briefcase he carried onto the credenza. "Why do you ask?"

"Because I'd like to know."

He eyed Michael. "Because had I told you to go after her, you'd have run for the hills. I see my reverse psychology did the trick." His father's eyes, blue like his own, sparkled.

"We've got to get through the Fairmont case. I just hope that she can handle losing. It's as important to her as it is to me."

"Let me tell you something, Mike. That gal is a businesswoman."

Michael got out of Jason's chair and stood at the door. "Just for the record, I'd have liked her even if you'd given me the go-ahead."

Jason sat down in the chair Mike vacated. "Just for the record, I doubt it. Remember Sharon Garrett. Your mother and I were so excited when you brought her home. You let her get away, though, didn't you?"

"No. We just never thought about each other in a romantic way."

"How does the Price girl feel about you?"

"Just when I think she likes me, she does a one-eighty."

"That sounds about right. Good luck. I'd like to see grandchildren, you know."

Joe Fairmont stood at the door of Michael's office with Joey on a leash. "So, when is Sallie due home?"

Michael got up from his chair and faced Joe. "I'm not sure, I could call Miss Price and ask her."

Michael saw the wheels in Joe's mind

turning. "That won't be necessary." He handed the lead to Michael, who without thinking took it.

"You just tell her she can babysit until her client gets home."

"You can't leave the pig with me."

"I'm not. I'm telling you to take him to that little prissy lawyer of Sallie's. Let her see what it takes to care for him and decide if Sallie really will do it."

Before Michael could protest more, Joe was gone.

He checked his watch. By the time he could get to Danni's she would probably be home. He grabbed his suit jacket and left his office, with Joey leading the way.

Getting him in the car wasn't at all hard. Obviously, Joey liked to ride. The little guy even rolled down the passenger side window by using his hoof on the automatic window switch.

His intelligence overwhelmed Michael who wondered what it must have looked like to the other drivers, his sports car with a pig's snout hanging out the window as they ventured down the road.

When they reached Danni's house, her

car was in the driveway. A good sign she was at home.

He and Joey got out of the car and walked onto the front porch. When he rang the bell, he could hear her dog barking and hoped Lilly wouldn't see the pig as a roast of pork when it entered the house.

Danni opened the door. Her eyes became wide upon seeing Michael and wider when she realized Joey accompanied him.

"What are you doing with Joey?"

"Long story, counselor. May we come in?"

She backed away to allow them to do so.

Lilly sniffed at the other animal, and licked him on his snout.

"I think they'll be okay, while he's here." Michael didn't let go of his leash.

"I need to put her out, anyway. C'mon, Lilly. Let's go out."

The dog was ready to do so, in fact, Joey tried to follow, but Michael kept him close by.

Danni returned to find Michael sitting on the couch, Joey at his side.

"What's going on, Mike? Why do you have our clients' property? In fact, I thought you were no longer representing

Fairmont." Danni sat down in one of the chairs opposite the couch. She wore shorts and a knit top.

"Well, that's a good story, Danni. I guess I'll just cut to the chase, however. Joe changed his mind about sacking me. He's finished with his commercial. Sallie's out of town. Joe expects you to care for Joey until your client is back—"

"And, you brought the little guy here? I can't care for him, I know nothing about potbellied pigs!"

"You and me both." Michael's eyes held surprise and he looked down. "So *that's* why you were so anxious to follow Lilly outside." His shoes were covered in a wet mess.

Joey only snorted as if to say, "I told you so."

"My yard is fenced in, let me put him out and get you a towel."

"I think he's finished," Michael groaned.

With no further discussion, Danni took Joey outside. She waited at the door for a moment after unleashing him to make sure he and Lilly would be agreeable, but they lay down together in a shady spot and

Danni saw no reason to continue to monitor them.

Inside, Michael was already in her bathroom and she could hear water running. She let him alone and went into the kitchen to pour them both a glass of lemonade.

When she brought the tray to the table that sat outside of her kitchen on the second floor balcony, Michael came out of the bathroom.

"We'll sit here, for now."

He pulled up a chair. "Thanks."

"What are we supposed to do with the pig, Michael?"

He sipped his drink and put the glass down. "I have no idea. I suppose we could kennel him."

"No. He's an important pig, in the grand scheme of things. After all, if we were to lose him, somehow, we'd be losing the spokesperson for Fairmont Farms, not just another pet."

Michael nodded in agreement. "I have an idea, though. Do you have a computer?"

Danni showed him into the bedroom she'd fixed as her home office. Filing cabinets, and her computer, along with a few plants to keep the place from looking sterile. She sat down in front of the computer and turned it on.

"Go online." Michael smiled. "There's two ways to skin a cat, or pig, as in our situation."

Once she'd found a page on potbellied pigs, Michael—who looked over her shoulder—and she read about the animals. It would have been much easier for her had they not been in such close proximity.

Michael stood up straight and flexed his back after bending over for so many minutes. "We know that he's intelligent, can be housebroken, and needs to be told who the boss is."

Danni looked back over her shoulder to Michael. "Then, we need to decide who the boss is, don't we?"

"I'm sorry, Danni, but unless you want me to spend the night, I can't keep the pig. My super would have a fit."

Danni refused to allow thoughts of Michael in her home overnight. Instead, she tried to be indignant about the fact that she'd be the one who had to keep the extra animal for the weekend. "The article said that he could become aggressive about food and that he might root in my yard."

"Which, may I add, is better than what he did on my foot."

Danni turned off the computer and stood up to walk back to the table.

Michael moved out of her way and followed her. "I know what you're thinking."

"This isn't fair."

"I know. But, the only other option we have is a kennel."

"Which won't work, under the circumstances."

They both sat at the table, quiet for a moment.

"Michael, what do pigs eat?"

"I think the article said we could pick up pig food."

"At the local convenience store? It's late in the day and there's nothing I can think of that pigs eat, except maybe corn?"

"Where did you come up with corn?"

"I saw it once in a cartoon."

Michael laughed. "I can see you now, in the courtroom saying, 'I think that after seeing a coyote fall from a much taller height, it only reasonable my client to think he could push the victim from a twenty story building without killing him, Your

Honor.' I'd love to see you as a criminal attorney."

"Oh, but aren't we funny?" Danielle chided. "For one moment, Uncle Miltie—or Mikie—as the case may be, if you can put your humor on hold, I have an idea."

"Should we call the rabbit and ask his advice?"

"Better yet, let's call one of the big pet stores, maybe they'd have something in stock."

Within the hour, Michael had gone to the pet store, brought back pig food, and made himself at home on her couch watching a ball game. Joey lay in the floor at his feet, eating pig food and grunting a happy noise.

Lilly wandered a little too close and Joey made it clear whose food he ate. So, she jumped back to the chair where she normally sat when Danni left her office long enough to indulge in a little television.

Danni knew that she couldn't continue to engage in this fantasy of Michael in her home, with dog and pig at their sides, but it did feel nice, even if just for a few hours.

Joey got up and waddled to the door. He scratched at it with his little cloven hoof.

"I understand him." Michael winked at

her as he beckoned Joey to follow him. "It's a guy thing."

Lilly followed Joey out the back door and into the yard. Danni now recognized the call of nature when she saw it.

Michael closed the door behind them. "You know, counselor, with the children away, the adults could play."

"I have no checkers, Mr. Sommers."

He edged closer to her. "Chess?"

"I think not. Anyway, I can handle one little pig for the night."

At that very moment, all hell broke lose, squealing and barking and dirt flying everywhere. Michael, with Danni right behind him, ran out to save Joey. But, when they ran the few steps into the backyard, they realized it was Lilly who'd treaded too close to the food that Michael had put out for Joey earlier.

Danni brought Lilly in the house for a few minutes to allow both animals to gather their wits.

"Rule number two: be careful about Joey with Lilly when food is involved." Danni put the dog on her lap and continued to pet her.

"Sure you don't want me on the couch this weekend?"

"Positive. I can take care of myself and two animals who at least aren't supposed to be as wise as I am."

Other than a quick good-bye, Michael left with no further discussion. Danni couldn't help but wish he'd offered to come back later, or something. But, she knew that this all led down an impossible road.

A road she didn't want to travel only to find heartache at the end.

"I am not settling for a penny less, either." Sallie Fairmont had returned from her cruise ready to defend her honor and her pig. She decided on twice her original figure.

"I can't get you that money, Sallie. It won't happen." She told her the last figure she gave Michael.

"You aren't serious? After all he tried to do to me? Oh, no. He's bought my wrath now. That's not enough." The Sallie who tried to convince Danni she was a righteous, upstanding citizen was gone.

"Sallie, I know you think you're looking

good right now, but let me explain. You have a newscaster that has called you everything except a tramp. She has tried every way in the world to destroy you. You don't know whose side the Judge will be on. He may read *The Hometowner*, but I doubt it. He may watch Channel Seven, or he may watch Channel Eleven. We can't test the waters. All we can do is settle."

"You're a great attorney, Miss Price. I want to go for everything. If you can't double it then by all means, do something."

Danni thought about what her client said. "Fine. We'll go for it. But, don't be surprised if we end up in court."

"Who cares? The paper made me look like a queen."

"And, Channel Seven made you look like something out of the gutter. As your attorney, I recommend we take the final offer and be happy. It's a fair deal, Sallie."

Sallie got up from her chair. "I'll think about it."

After she left, Michael called on Danni. She told her secretary to show him right in.

Michael sat down at Danni's wave to the chair. "There is no offer on the table, Dan-

ielle. Joe refuses to give his ex-wife anything."

After a long moment, Danni spoke.
"Then, we go to court."

He nodded. "To court it is."

"This isn't what I'd hoped. I've talked to
her until I'm hoarse."

Michael's tone left her no doubt he had
done the same with his client. "I know. Joe
and I have gone round and round. How's
the Winters case coming?"

"Not bad. Things are moving along at a
snail's pace as originally planned."

Michael lowered his gaze. "I know you
put yourself on the line for me, Danni."

"Yep. I guess that's enough of the 'just
another attorney' theory." She didn't know
how to make her next sentence sound
pleasant. "There *is* good news. Mr. Greene
doesn't realize I did. He thinks I really tried
to destroy you."

Confusion wrote itself along Michael's
handsome face. "Somehow I find that com-
forting, which is actually scary."

Danni couldn't help but change to *the*
subject. "Sharon invited me to the wedding."

Michael didn't miss a beat. "Really? When did you see her?"

"A few days ago at the courthouse. She sang *your* praises." She wanted him to know how Sharon felt, so he would . . . do what? Quit asking *her* out? Or maybe, break it off with Sharon so she could have him.

He grinned. "The wedding is all she talks about."

"I'm not sure about coming. I think it would be awkward."

"Well, I *will* be there."

"That goes without saying."

"And, if Sharon invited you, she really wants you to come. She's not the type who does things just to be polite."

"You wouldn't have a problem with me being there?"

"No, not at all. Who knows, maybe you'll catch the bouquet."

Danni thought, *this is ludicrous.* "I really need to get back to work. Good luck, and all that."

"You too. I guess we'll see each other when depositions begin." With that and a nod, he was gone.

Chapter Thirteen

Had it only been twenty-four hours since she and Michael had spoken? Danni removed the keys from her pocket and opened her office door.

Sallie Fairmont opened the door to the lobby. Every hair in perfect place, every nail manicured. "Have you heard?"

Not again. "Heard what?"

"You haven't, then. Some little known animal organization that monitors the treatment of animals has hit the family business. They feel our fight for Joey is wrong and is asking for a boycott of Fairmont Farms products. You take that last offer and you take it now!"

Danni turned back to her office and made her way to the phone. She dialed Sommers, Sommers, and Cole. "Michael Sommers, please."

He answered.

"This is Danielle Price, have you decided to take my final offer on the Fairmont case?"

"Which 'final' offer would that *be*, Danni?"

She named the last figure she'd asked for in their previous negotiations.

She knew from the sound of his voice that Michael was amazed.

"We'll take it. I'll send the papers over. God, what a relief."

"Very true. Thank you, Mr. Sommers."

He paused. "Your client there?"

"That's correct." Her voice stayed a cool and business-like tone.

His comment came more as a question. "Oh. Okay, then I'll talk to you after she leaves?"

"Yes, I'll take care of that."

"I'll wait here for your call."

She hung up the phone to see Sallie staring at her in complete angst.

"It's done," Danni told her, "The paperwork should be ready by noon tomorrow."

Sallie sighed with obvious relief. "Thank God. Let me know when I can have the money, will you?"

Sallie breezed out in the same quick manner she'd come into the office.

Danni slowly picked up her phone to call Michael back. She dialed the number with unhurried and deliberate accuracy, not wanting to speak to him, but knowing this had to be completed.

Michael answered his phone then asked Danni, "Sallie heard about the animal group, didn't she?"

Danni sat down in the chair behind her desk. "Yes, she did. I'm surprised you hadn't let me know that."

"I just found out myself. Joe called not ten minutes before you did, and asked me to settle."

Danni sighed. "So, it's over."

"Yep," Michael agreed, "Seems so."

She didn't know what to do next. She hated this ambivalence of not wanting to break the tie between them and knowing he had to be let loose. "Then, I'll send my secretary over and we'll get this ended."

Michael, too, sounded unsure. "All settled and wrapped up in a neat little bow." Michael paused. When he did speak, he sounded almost angry. "So, is this it? Is this all there is?"

Danni, surprised at his change of posture, held her ground. Though she admitted she didn't know why. "Are you copping an attitude, Michael?"

His sarcastic answer left her unimpressed. "Oh, no. I'd never do that. Well, I guess I'll see you in court, then."

She hung up the phone, seething. "He's not getting to me like this. I won't allow it."

Saturday loomed before Danni as a sentence of boredom. At only eleven o'clock she'd already done all the housework she wanted to do and planted a few tulips outside.

There's more to life than this.

She wanted to go on a drive with Michael in his sports car. She wanted the top down. She wanted the wind on her face.

But, that wouldn't happen. Last Friday,

all the paperwork was signed, sealed, and delivered. Not one word from him, only a nod from the courier who delivered the final papers.

How stupid could one woman be? She knew him. She knew who he was, his reputation, his fiancée. She knew it all, but her heart wasn't easily controlled by her mind.

"I shouldn't be allowed out without a keeper," she told Lilly who lay at her feet as Danni reached down to rub her belly.

"You know, Lilly. I may just start letting you sleep inside, since it seems you're the only company I'm ever going to have, anyway."

She heard the mailman opening the box and allowed him to leave before she checked the mail.

The invitation. She held it in her hand, and the burning sensation, only an illusion she knew, didn't go away as she stared at it. *Not that. Anything but that.* She couldn't stand that. She couldn't open this and keep from slitting her wrists when she read it.

She couldn't.

Or could she? After all, she now had a successful career, her own home, a dog . . .

but that was all. In her hand, she held the proof that Michael would never be hers.

Before she realized she'd done it, the envelope was torn open and she read the words. Michael's name was nowhere to be found on the card. She double-checked it over and over.

Reality hit her hard.

Her situation had nothing to do with Sharon Garrett, who—according to the invitation—was marrying a man named Frank Donovan.

Michael just didn't want her.

She sat down on the couch, patted it so Lilly would do the one thing she loved and never got to, she jumped up to sit beside Danni.

"It's just you and me, Lilly." She rubbed the dog's tummy. Through tears, she repeated, "It's just you and me."

The doorbell rang, which was probably good as Danni was talking to dogs and herself.

She opened the door. "Michael! What in the world?"

He not only stood on her doorstep live and in person but had a friend with him.

She eyed the pretty little pig. "This can't be Joey? I mean, I thought Joe had him."

Michael smiled. "May we come in?"

"Of course. My word, what's going on? Why do you have him?"

Michael didn't sit down, and kept Joey on his leash. "We're here to argue our case."

Confusion coursed through her. "Your case?"

"Yes, counselor. I have with me the defense's exhibit one."

"Okay, I'll bite." Even dressed in shorts and a T-shirt, she put on her best courtroom voice, "Go ahead, Mr. Sommers."

"I have with me a pig. A very cute and cuddly pig, by the way. One that will make some happy couple a very nice little pig. He gets along well with dogs, as the defense will show."

"To hang out here, he'd have to love dogs."

Mike let go of Joey's leash. When he did so, Joey and Lilly chased each other barking and squealing. They were a show of perfect harmony when they tired and lay down together after sharing some water from Lilly's dish.

Danni crossed her arms over her chest. "Your point is taken, Mr. Sommers. Please continue."

"In the light that Mr. and Mrs. Fairmont have each decided they no longer need Joey to torture each other, or for the ad campaign which lost its following after Joey was put on the news, I am now his father."

Danni eyed Mike for a moment.

"I'm not going to lie to you, Danni. Joey needs a mother."

She pursed her lips. "Oh, I get it, so let's pawn the pig on Danni, right?"

"No, not at all. Let's get married and give him a real home."

"I just got Sharon's invitation. She isn't marrying you."

"You thought I was engaged to Sharon? All this time, you thought I was chasing you and engaged to another woman? No wonder I almost never caught you."

"But, she told me how wonderful you are."

Michael took her in his arms. "Well, honey, of course she did. She wanted you to like me because I told her I'm in love with you."

Danni relaxed. Her dreams could come true, after all. "So, let me see what I get in this great bargain. A cute guy, whose father probably hates me, and who comes with his own pig."

"My father thinks you're great. He and Grand Dad, in fact, want you to work with us to avoid conflicts of interest in the future. The pig part, however, is on the mark. I've gotten attached to the little ham." Joey snorted from the corner as he turned over to his other side.

"I love you, Danielle B. Price. I love you."

"I love you, too. And, Danni will do fine. But, I'm not leaving my job, not even for you. I've worked hard and now that I've come into my own, I'm going to keep it."

His warm lips found hers, sending a thrill through her entire body.

"We'll work it out. You can work wherever you want, as long as you love me. By the way," Michael wanted to know, "What's the B for?"

Danni couldn't look him in the eye, so kept her gaze on the top button of his shirt, "Well, you may as well know. It's my grandmother's maiden name."

"Oh?"

"Boone."

"Your name is *Danielle Boone*?"

"My darkest secret." She looked up at him. "I must really love you."

He pulled her back into their embrace and whispered, "Love me, love my pig."

"You got it."